THE
PLANET
HUNTERS

For Clyde and Patsy Tombaugh

The author thanks his wife, Judith Bloom Fradin,
and their daughter, Diana Judith Fradin, for research assistance

THE
PLANET
HUNTERS

THE SEARCH FOR OTHER WORLDS

Dennis Brindell Fradin

Illustrated with full-color and black-and-white prints and photographs

MARGARET K. McELDERRY BOOKS

MARGARET K. McELDERRY BOOKS
25 YEARS • 1972–1997

Margaret K. McElderry Books
An imprint of Simon & Schuster
Children's Publishing Division
1230 Avenue of the Americas
New York, New York 10020

Book design by Patti Ratchford
The text of this book was set in Janson Text.
Printed in the United States of America
First Edition
10 9 8 7 6 5 4 3 2 1

Library of Congress Cataloging-in-Publication
Data
Fradin, Dennis B.
The planet hunters : the search for other worlds /
Dennis Brindell Fradin.
p. cm.
Includes bibliographical references and index.
Summary: provides historical information on
astronomy, the discovery of the planets, and the
people who have made such discoveries.
ISBN 0-689-81323-6
1. Astronomers—Juvenile literature.
2. Astronomy—History—Juvenile literature.
3. Planets—History—Juvenile literature.
[1. Astronomers. 2. Astronomy—History.
3. Planets—History.] I. Title.
QB35.F73 1997
523.4—dc21
96-29721
CIP AC

THE AUTHOR THANKS THE FOLLOWING INDIVIDUALS FOR THEIR ASSISTANCE:

Dr. Anita Cochran, Astronomy Department, University of Texas at Austin

Dr. William Cochran, Astronomy Department, University of Texas at Austin

Dr. Mike Davis, senior research associate, Arecibo Observatory

Bettie Greber, executive director, Space Studies Institute

Douglas Isbell, Public Affairs Officer, NASA

Charles Kowal, operations astronomer, Space Telescope Science Institute

Dr. Mark Littmann, Journalism and Astronomy Departments, University of Tennessee at Knoxville

Dr. Jane Luu, professor of astronomy, Harvard University

Dr. Richard Muller, Department of Physics, University of California at Berkeley

Andy Perala, Keck Observatory

Venetia Burney Phair

Dr. Conley Powell, aerospace engineer, Teledyne Brown Engineering

Don Savage, Public Affairs Officer, NASA

Jim Seevers, astronomer, the Adler Planetarium of Chicago

Seth Shostak, astronomer, the SETI Institute

Dr. John Stansberry, planetary scientist, Lowell Observatory

Clyde and Patsy Tombaugh

Dr. Tom Van Flandern, astronomer, University of Maryland at College Park

Dr. Daniel P. Whitmire, professor of physics, University of Louisiana at Lafayette

Dr. Alex Wolszczan, Astronomy Department, Penn State University

❊ CONTENTS ❊

NUMBERS USED IN THIS BOOK

* one hundred = 100

* one thousand = 1,000

* one million = 1,000,000

* one billion = 1,000,000,000

* one trillion = 1,000,000,000,000

* one sextillion = 1,000,000,000,000,000,000,000

* a zillion = an imaginary number people use to express a huge but unknown amount, as in the expression "zillions of stars"

* astronomical unit – a unit often used to measure distances in the Solar System; one astronomical unit is 93 million miles, the average distance between the Earth and the Sun

* century = a period of 100 years

* speed of light = 186,282 miles per second

* light-year = the distance light travels in a year, 5,880,000,000,000 (5.88 trillion) miles

* millisecond = a thousandth of a second

◑ Many astronomers use the metric system to express distances, speeds, and temperatures.

◑ Metric distances and speeds are measured in kilometers rather than miles. One kilometer = .62 of a mile, and one mile = 1.61 kilometers.

◑ Metric temperatures are measured on the Celsius (C.) rather than the Fahrenheit (F.) scale. To convert Fahrenheit to Celsius, subtract 32 degrees from the F. temperature, then multiply the remainder by 5/9 or .555. To change Celsius to Fahrenheit, multiply the C. temperature by 9/5 or 1.8, then add 32 degrees to the product.

Below are some astronomical distances, speeds, and temperatures converted into kilometers and degrees Celsius.

◑ Distance of Moon from Earth—about 240,000 miles (about 385,000 kilometers)

◑ Distance of Earth from Sun—about 93 million miles (about 150 million kilometers)

◑ Distance of Jupiter from Sun—about 500 million miles (about 800 million kilometers)

◑ Diameter of Ceres—about 600 miles (about 1,000 kilometers)

◑ Diameter of Pluto—about 1,400 miles (about 2,250 kilometers)

METRIC MEASUREMENTS

- Diameter of Earth—7,926 miles (12,760 kilometers)

- Diameter of Jupiter—about 89,000 miles (about 143,300 kilometers)

- Speed of light—186,282 miles per second (approximately 300,000 kilometers per second)

- One light-year—5,880,000,000,000 or 5.88 trillion miles (9,500,000,000,000 or 9.5 trillion kilometers)

- Distance to nearest star, Proxima Centauri—25 trillion miles (40 trillion kilometers), but generally expressed by astronomers as 4.3 light-years

- Freezing point of water on Earth—32^0 F. (0^0 C.)

- Boiling point of water on Earth—212^0 F. (100^0 C.)

- Average temperature on Earth—57^0 F. (14^0 C.)

- High temperature on Mars—about 65^0 F. (about 18^0 C.)

- Low temperature on Mars—about -220^0 F. (about -140^0 C.)

- Estimated temperature of planet of 51 Peg—$1,800^0$ F. (about $1,000^0$ C.)

- Temperature of Sun's surface—about $10,000^0$ F. (about $5,500^0$ C.)

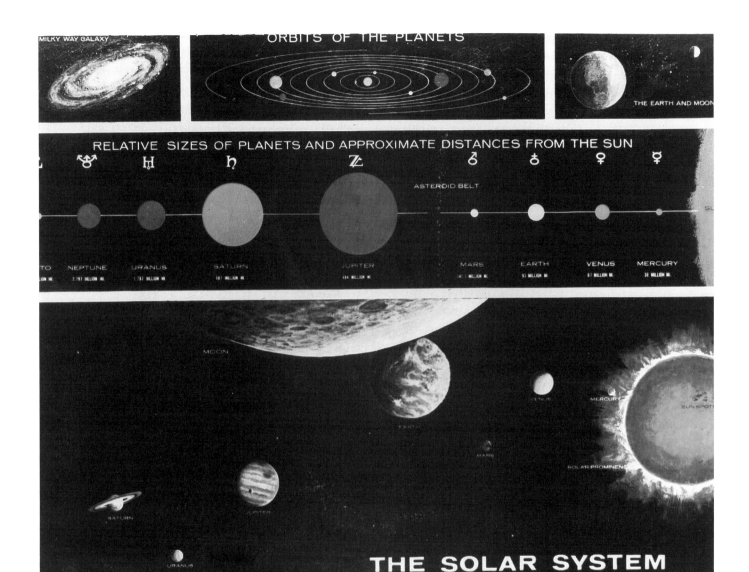

Artist's view of (top left) the Milky Way Galaxy, in which our Sun is located, as it might appear from afar; (top center) the planets orbiting the Sun; (top right) our Earth and Moon as seen from space; (middle) the relative sizes of, right to left, the Sun, Mercury, Venus, Earth, Mars, Jupiter, Saturn, Uranus, Neptune, and Pluto; (bottom) several objects in the Solar System as seen from behind the Moon.

ONE

THE FIVE "WANDERERS" OF THE ANCIENT SKIES

Aristarchus was accused of evil teachings. He refused to acknowledge that the Earth is at the center of the Universe. Instead, he claimed that it moves in an orbit [around the Sun] and at the same time spins on its axis.

Ancient description of the Greek astronomer
Aristarchus, who lived about 2,300 years ago

✳ On a clear night, in a place far from city lights, a person with good vision can see about 3,000 stars in the sky. A few stars are so bright that they dazzle the eye, but many others are barely visible. There are white stars and blue stars, orange stars and red stars, yellow stars and stars that seem to change color as they twinkle. Many people who view the star-filled sky for the first time are almost hypnotized by its splendor. Whether children or adults, they are likely to wonder: How many stars are there and how far away are they? Do stars extend forever in space or is there a place where they end? Are we alone in the Universe, or do beings on other worlds look up at their night sky with the same sense of awe that we feel? (Figure 1)

People have undoubtedly asked these questions for most of our two million years on Earth. Some of the oldest known relics created by human beings have astronomical significance. Ten thousand–year-old bones on which people recorded the cycles of the Moon have been found in Africa and Europe. Cliff drawings and stone monuments found in many places also prove that people have been intrigued by the objects in the heavens since prehistoric times.

Our ancient ancestors observed that seven celestial objects behave differently than the stars in the night sky. One of them, the huge yellow orb we call the Sun, appears only by day and seems to take the light away when it sets each evening. The second unusual object was the large body we call the Moon, which seems to change shape during a cycle lasting about thirty days. (Figure 2)

The other five unusual objects resemble bright stars, yet differ from them in two important ways. First, a star twinkles "like a diamond in the sky," as the nursery rhyme says, while the five special objects shine with a steady light. Also, the relative positions of the stars change so slowly over long periods of time that the ancients made up imaginary star pictures called constellations that look nearly the same today as they did thousands of years ago. On the other hand, the five unusual objects do not remain in fixed positions, but move through the constellations from month to month and year to year.

Ancient people generally worshiped the seven unusual heavenly bodies as gods and goddesses. The Greeks believed that the Sun was the god Helios and the Moon his sister Selene. They referred to the five bright objects that moved among the constellations as *planetae*, meaning "wanderers." Although the Greeks did not understand the nature of the "wanderers," their word *planetae* lives on in our modern name for the objects: *planets*.

The Romans coined the names still applied to the five known planets of ancient times. The fast-moving orange planet that always remained near the Sun they named *Mercury*, for their fleet-footed

The constellation Ursa Major (the Great Bear), also known as the Big Dipper.

messenger of the gods who wore magic sandals. The brilliant white planet that outshone every heavenly body except the Sun and the Moon they called *Venus,* for their goddess of love. The red planet reminded the Romans of blood, so they named it *Mars,* for their god of war. The yellow planet that wandered slowly through the constellations the Romans named *Jupiter,* for their king of the gods who was also known as Jove. The golden planet that moved even more slowly than Jupiter they named *Saturn,* for Jupiter's father. The Romans worshiped the Moon as Luna, a goddess who drove across the night

The gods and goddesses for whom the days of the week were named. From right they are
Saturn (Saturday), the Sun (Sunday), the Moon (Monday), Mars (Tuesday), Mercury
(Wednesday), Jupiter (Thursday), and Venus (Friday).

sky in her chariot, and identified the Sun with Apollo, the god of musicians and poets.

Other people had their own beliefs about the seven special heavenly bodies. To the people of ancient India the Sun was Surya, a god who was driven across the sky by a seven-headed horse. The ancient Egyptians believed that the planets Mars, Jupiter, and Saturn were various forms of Horus, a god with a man's body and a bird's head. The Babylonians, who lived in what is now Iraq, worshiped Jupiter as Marduk, their king of the gods who killed a dragon and created the sky and the oceans out of its body. Mexico's Maya and Aztec Indians referred to Venus as Quetzalcoatl, a god who also took the form of a feathered serpent. The Masai people of Africa claimed that the Sun and the Moon were a husband and wife who had a fight. The Sun god was so ashamed of his bruises that he made himself bright to keep people from looking at him, but when we gaze upon the Moon goddess's face, we can see her injuries. (Figure 3)

Ancient Jewish people did not associate the heavenly bodies with gods and goddesses, for their religion, Judaism, taught that there is only one God. Yet they believed that each planet influenced a part of the human body and a day of the week. For example, Mars was associated with the right ear and the day we call Tuesday, and Mercury's influence extended to the left nostril and Friday. The Chinese identified each planet with an important substance. They called Mercury *Shui Xing*, the Water Star, and Venus *Jin Xing*, the Gold Star. The red planet, Mars, was *Huo Xing*, the Fire Star, while Jupiter was *Mu Xing*, the Wood Star, and Saturn was *Tu Xing*, the Earth Star.

The Moon, Sun, and five planets known to the ancients influenced our language, calendar, and other aspects of our daily life. Seven is considered a lucky number to this day because of the seven unusual heavenly bodies, and the week has seven days for the same reason. Each of our days is named for one of the objects. *Sunday* and *Monday* are old words meaning "the Sun's Day" and "the Moon's Day." *Tuesday*, *Wednesday*, and *Thursday* come from old words meaning "the Day of Mars," "the Day of Mercury," and "the Day of Jupiter." *Friday* is "the Day of Venus," and *Saturday* is "Saturn's Day."

Helium, an element used to fill balloons, was named for the Sun god, Helios. Because the god and planet Mercury moved so quickly, the element used in thermometers was named mercury, and individuals whose moods quickly change are called "mercurial." People who are gloomy or slow to act are sometimes described as "saturnine" for the slow-moving planet, while good-natured individuals are called "jovial" in honor of Saturn's son, King Jupiter or Jove. Long ago, nations took time out from wars during the winter, because the cold weather could claim more lives than the battles. They resumed fighting when the weather turned warmer, which was why the first month of spring was named *March* for Mars, the god of war.

The Moon inspired the custom of dividing the year into twelve segments. Each of these periods roughly corresponds to the Moon's thirty-day cycle and is called a *month*, a word related to *Mene*, meaning "Moon" in Greek. The Moon also figures in many old superstitions, including the belief that it could transform people into werewolves or wolf-men. To this day, mentally ill people are sometimes called *lunatics*, as a result of the ancient belief that the Moon and its goddess, Luna, could do strange things to the human mind.

Except for a handful of individuals considered in their own time to be lunatics, ancient people shared a completely false view of the Universe. They thought that all of the heavenly bodies circled the Earth, which stood motionless at the center of everything. There seemed to be a simple "proof" of this. At night the Moon, stars, and planets traveled across the sky in an arc from east to west, and each day the Sun did the same. (Figure 4) All a person had to do was watch a planet rise over a treetop in the east or a star set behind a mountain in the west to see "evidence" that the heavenly bodies circled the Earth from east to west.

The Greek astronomer Aristarchus was one of the very few ancient scientists who differed with this theory. About 2,300 years ago, Aristarchus claimed that the heavenly bodies only *appear* to circle overhead because our Earth spins like a top. He also suggested that the Earth orbits the Sun—not the other way around. Aristarchus was accurate on both counts, but for many centuries his ideas were ridiculed.

Ptolemy, a Greek astronomer who was born about 100 A.D., led the attack on Aristarchus's theories. "If the Earth actually rotated to the east," reasoned Ptolemy, "wouldn't winds always blow westward and clouds always move westward?" Ptolemy became the most famous spokesman for the false idea that the Earth stands still and is the center of the Universe, a theory that became known as the "Ptolemaic System." Its followers, called "Ptolemaists," developed numerous arguments to explain why the Earth couldn't possibly spin. One was

Ptolemy, whose theory of an Earth-centered Universe was accepted for many centuries.

that a spinning Earth would make us feel constantly dizzy. They also argued that if the Earth really rotated, a rock or ball hurled into the sky would be left far behind rather than coming down near where it was thrown.

One thing disturbed the Ptolemaists, however. Certain movements of the planets could best be explained if in fact they orbited the Sun rather than the Earth. At times some planets make backward loops in the sky. This *retrograde motion* is due to the Earth overtaking the other "wanderers" as the planets all orbit the Sun, much as a car traveling 50 miles per hour on a highway can appear to be moving backward if you are whizzing past it at 60 miles per hour. Ptolemy concocted another explanation for the planets' backward loops. He claimed that the planets travel in large circles around the Earth, but that they sometimes also move in extra small circles called *epicycles*. Although completely wrong, this explanation won acceptance because it accounted for the retrograde motion of the "wanderers" while keeping the Earth standing still at the center of the Universe.

The Ptolemaic System reigned virtually unchallenged for nearly 1,400 years. During those fourteen centuries the Earth spun like a top (as Aristarchus claimed) half a million times, Mercury orbited the Sun five thousand times, and Saturn made fifty trips around the Sun—yet all the while humanity continued to believe that we stood motionless at the center of creation.

TWO

THE DISCOVERY OF PLANET EARTH

And so, as if seated upon a royal throne, the Sun rules the family of the planets as they orbit around him. What a picture—so simple, so clear, so beautiful!

Nicholas Copernicus, *Concerning the Revolutions of the Heavenly Spheres* (1543)

✸ According to an old saying, people who overlook the obvious "can't see the nose in front of their face." This expression is fitting for the discovery of our own planet. Although they are millions of miles from Earth, the planets Mercury, Venus, Mars, Jupiter, and Saturn have been known since antiquity. But it took human beings until recent centuries to realize that the Earth on which we live is a planet, too.

After the death of Ptolemy, few advances in science were made for well over a thousand years. In fact, the Middle Ages of European history (approximately 400 to 1400 A.D.) are also called the Dark Ages because ignorance and superstition were so widespread. During those years little was accomplished in astronomy—the scientific study of stars, planets, and other heavenly bodies. Yet a pseudoscience (false science) called *astrology* flourished.

Astrology is based on the notion that the positions of the planets and other celestial objects contain secrets for predicting future events

People had little understanding of the Universe during the Middle Ages. In this woodcut, a man is poking his head through the starry dome of the sky into the unknown.

in people's lives. Kings and queens of the Middle Ages consulted astrologers to determine the luckiest times to be crowned. Other people delayed their weddings or even refused to go outside or bathe because the planets were supposedly in unlucky positions for them. To the astrologers of long ago, a conjunction (the appearance of two or more planets close together in the sky) foretold disaster. A planetary conjunction in the year 1186 convinced astrologers that a giant storm was coming, prompting people to dig underground shelters. No catastrophe occurred, yet there were similar false predictions in 1229, 1236, 1339, 1371, and 1395.

The Renaissance, a period of renewed interest in learning, began in Europe around the year 1400. Great artworks were created, medicine advanced, but several generations of astronomers came and went and the Ptolemaic System remained unopposed. Meanwhile, astrology became more popular than ever. Perhaps the greatest astrological panic in history took place in 1524, when a series of planetary conjunctions occurred in the constellation Pisces the Fishes. Since Pisces was a "watery sign," astrologers predicted a worldwide flood. Many people, including a French university president, built arks or boats in the hope of surviving the deluge, just like Noah had in the Bible. A number of terrified people scrambling up hills to escape the flood were trampled to death. When the disaster failed to materialize, people sheepishly descended from the hilltops, and the French university president claimed that his ark was just a fishing boat.

Palmistry, a false science related to astrology, was also popular during the Renaissance. Its followers believed that the Sun, Moon, and planets revealed people's destiny through shapes and marks on their hands. In palmistry, the little finger was known as the "Mercury finger," the ring finger as the "Sun finger," the middle finger as the "Saturn finger," and the index finger as the "Jupiter finger." Other areas of the hand included the Mount of Venus, the Plain of Mars, and the Mount of the Moon. Palm readers claimed that people with long Mercury fingers tended to be moody and change their minds often, while those with high Mounts of Venus were warm and loving. Individuals with long Jupiter fingers supposedly had good leadership potential, but people with raised Plains of Mars had a tendency toward violence. Many people went through life convinced that their destiny was written in the sky and on their hands.

The man who led astronomy into the light was born on February 19, 1473, in Thorn (now Torun), Poland. Few people today know him by his original name: Nicholas Koppernigk. His father, a merchant and magistrate in Thorn, died when Nicholas was ten. The boy was adopted by his uncle, a priest and scholar who was so stern and saturnine that it was said he was never known to laugh. His uncle provided Nicholas with the best education the world could offer, sending him to universities until he was thirty-three years old.

Nicholas's higher education began when he was eighteen at the university in Krakow, Poland. At the time, it was a custom for scholars to coin Latin names for themselves. While in Krakow, Nicholas Koppernigk changed his last name to the Latin form by which he is remembered: Copernicus. Among his subjects, Nicholas Copernicus studied the Ptolemaic System of astronomy. But during Nicholas's student days in Krakow, there was a feeling of change in the air. In 1492, Christopher Columbus sailed westward across the Atlantic Ocean. Instead of being swallowed by sea monsters as people had predicted, Columbus discovered a New World. Writings from his student days show that by the age of twenty, Copernicus was beginning to doubt the Ptolemaic System and was entertaining Aristarchus's theory that the Earth orbits the Sun.

Nicholas's uncle rose to become a bishop in the Catholic Church. He decided that Nicholas should study Canon Law—the legal code governing the Church. After five years in Krakow's university, Nicholas spent ten years studying Canon Law at the Italian universities of Bologna, Padua, and Ferrara. At that time a Church official was expected to care for people's physical as well as spiritual needs, so Copernicus also studied medicine in Italy.

By 1506, when he was thirty-three years old, Copernicus had earned his Doctor of Canon Law degree. He spent the rest of his life working as a Church official called a *canon* and as a physician. It was

Nicholas Copernicus (1473–1543)

said that Copernicus was nicknamed the "Second Aesculapius" (for the Greek and Roman god of healing) because wherever the Church sent him in Poland, he treated the local poor people for free.

Meanwhile, Copernicus was developing a passion for astronomy. While stationed at Poland's Frauenburg Cathedral for a number of years, he lived in a tower overlooking the grounds. From his lofty vantage point, which became known as "Copernicus's Tower," he spent his nights observing the stars and planets. The telescope had not yet been invented, so he had no way to obtain close-up views of the heavenly bodies, but he measured their positions with a *triquetrum*, a device consisting of three rulers joined together.

Gradually Copernicus became convinced that the stars only appear to move across the sky because the Earth is spinning; that the Earth is a planet; and that it and the other planets orbit the Sun. He couldn't prove all of this, yet he felt it was the most logical explanation for the planets' retrograde motion. In about 1512 Copernicus wrote *Little Commentary*, in which he expressed his unorthodox astronomical ideas. At the time, people who published views that contradicted Church teachings could be labeled heretics, and risked being tortured or killed. For a Church official to claim that the Earth was not the center of the Universe would have been especially dangerous, so instead of publishing *Little Commentary* at one of the more than one thousand printing houses that had sprung up across Europe, Copernicus wrote out several copies of his booklet by hand and showed them to a few close friends.

Little Commentary was the seed of a much longer work that Copernicus spent thirty years writing and rewriting. In it, he presented his idea that the Earth is a planet similar to Venus or Mars and also countered the Ptolemaists' arguments. He answered their claim that an object thrown into the sky would be left behind if the Earth really spun by explaining that the air and the clouds rotate along with our planet. Copernicus's theory also explained that the Earth's spinning does not make us dizzy because our planet is so large.

Despite his massive writing efforts, Copernicus was as worried about publishing his long book as he had been about *Little Commentary.* For years, his manuscript remained locked in a drawer. Then, when he was in his late sixties, Copernicus realized that he had an obligation to share his information with the world. With the help of several friends, Nicholas Copernicus's book was published in the spring of 1543 on the last day of his life. A messenger rushed in to present the first printed copy to him as he lay dying. Shortly after looking at the volume, Copernicus passed away.

Copernicus's masterpiece, *Concerning the Revolutions of the Heavenly Spheres,* was one of the most important books ever written. May 24, 1543—the day of its publication and of Copernicus's death—can also be considered the day that planet Earth was discovered. For within its pages, *Revolutions* presented the best arguments that had ever been made that our Earth is a planet. In one passage, Copernicus wrote: "In the midst of all dwells the Sun. How could this light be given a better place to illuminate the whole temple of God? . . . Let it in truth guide the circling family of planets, including the Earth." More than 450 years later, teachers still use the concept of a family to describe the Solar System, which consists of the Sun and the many objects that orbit it, including the planets and their moons as well as comets and asteroids.

At first only a few highly educated people accepted the idea that the Earth was not the center of the Universe but was a planet like Mars or Jupiter. Most people considered the idea preposterous. Religious leaders were the fiercest foes of the "Copernican System." Martin Luther had begun a new division of Christianity called Protestantism in 1517, yet he wouldn't question the old view of the Universe. "The new astronomer wants to prove that the Earth, rather than the heavens, spins round," said Luther. "The fool will turn the whole science of Astronomy upside down!" For more than fifty years, the Catholic Church ignored *Revolutions,* viewing it as just a nuisance. But as the

Giordano Bruno (1548–1600)

book gradually gained followers, Church authorities denounced Copernicus's ideas. By the late 1500s, a professor who taught the Copernican System in a Catholic country was in danger of losing his job and even his life.

Giordano Bruno, an Italian monk and philosopher, ignored the order. He taught and wrote about the Copernican System, winning over thousands of converts. In his book *On the Infinite Universe and Worlds*, Bruno wrote: "In space there are countless suns and planets. We see only the suns because they give light. The planets remain invisible, for they are small and dark. There are also numberless Earths circling around their suns, no worse and no less inhabited than this globe of ours."

Bruno's description was remarkably close to our modern picture of the Universe, which is as follows: Scattered about space are many trillions of stars. These giant balls of hot, glowing gas appear to twinkle because they produce their own light and heat. The constellations hardly change over the ages because the stars comprising them are so distant that their motion appears slight to us. The Sun is an average star, and only looks so huge and bright compared to other stars because it is relatively nearby. Several planets, including Earth, orbit the Sun. The planets are much smaller than the Sun, which could hold more than a million Earths. Because they receive their light and heat from the Sun instead of generating these forms of energy themselves, the planets do not twinkle. They appear to wander through the constellations as they orbit the Sun because they are close to the Earth compared to the "background stars." Most of the planets, including Earth, are in turn orbited by smaller bodies called *moons*. Earth's lone Moon appears big and beautiful in our sky because it is the nearest heavenly body to us. As for Giordano Bruno's assertion that other stars besides the Sun also have planets, we are just now discovering this to be true—more than four hundred years after he proposed the idea.

For disagreeing with the Church on astronomical and other matters, Bruno was forced to leave Italy. He became a wandering philosopher who taught the Copernican System as he traveled through Europe. When he dared to return to Italy in 1591, he was imprisoned for nine years. All that time, Bruno refused to change his views and reportedly even told his judges: "I await your sentence with less fear than you pass it. The time will come when all will see what I see." Finally, he was sentenced to a gruesome death. On February 17, 1600, Giordano Bruno was led through the streets of Rome and then burned to death at the stake.

As Bruno predicted, the time came when the world accepted the Copernican System, but achieving this took nearly another hundred years of work by such scientists as Tycho Brahe, Johannes Kepler, Galileo Galilei, and Isaac Newton. Just as Copernicus was inspired by Aristarchus, and Bruno expanded on the Copernican System, these scientists built on each other's work. Newton acknowledged this with his famous comment: "If I have seen further than others, it was because I stood upon the shoulders of giants."

One of those giants, Tycho Brahe of Denmark, was born in 1546, when Copernicus's *Revolutions* had been out for three years. Tycho became intrigued by astronomy as a child, when he observed an eclipse that occurred as predicted. "To know such a thing in advance makes a man almost a god," he told his family. Tycho was expected to prepare for a political career, but he neglected his schoolwork to read about astronomy, and he was also too hot tempered to become a statesman.

Tycho Brahe (1546–1601)

At twenty, he fought a duel in which part of his nose was sliced off. After that, Tycho wore an artificial metal nose, but few people noticed because he slept by day and observed the sky by night. He achieved such fame as an astronomer that in 1576 the king of Denmark presented him with an observatory and estate on the island of Ven. Brahe named his domain *Uraniborg*, meaning "Castle of the Sky," and there he lived in a kind of splendor enjoyed by no astronomer before or since. With funds from the king, Brahe held lavish banquets, hired astronomical assistants, and built instruments for measuring star and planet positions, including a device that allowed him to observe the night sky while lying in bed.

Brahe's records of the heavenly bodies' movements were the most accurate that had been made up to that time. However, he made little use of his observations except to concoct a strange, muddled theory. Ptolemy and Copernicus were *both* partly right and partly wrong, he decided. According to Brahe, the planets Mercury, Venus, Mars, Jupiter, and Saturn circled the Sun as Copernicus claimed, but the Sun and stars circled the Earth as Ptolemy believed!

Continuing to argue with people, Brahe made so many enemies that he had to leave Denmark after the death of the king, his greatest supporter. He spent his last years in Prague, in what is now the Czech Republic, where he hired a German mathematician and astronomer named Johannes Kepler as his assistant. Kepler, who was supposed to help make observations, had the gall to inform Brahe that he preferred to calculate the orbits of planets rather than observe them. Earlier in life, Brahe would have exploded at the brash assistant, who was twenty-five years his junior. But Brahe had mellowed and he befriended Kepler, taking an almost fatherly interest in helping him with his career. Brahe also realized that he needed Kepler, for what good were his thousands of observations without someone who could interpret them? "I do not want to have lived in vain," Tycho Brahe said just before he died at the age of fifty-five in 1601. Because Brahe left his mountain of data to Kepler, his last wish came true.

Ironically, Kepler used the information Brahe had gathered over twenty years to disprove Tycho's theory. Siding with Copernicus, Kepler formulated his Three Laws of Planetary Motion to explain the movements of the planets according to the

Johannes Kepler (1571–1630)

Copernican System. They state that the planets' orbits are elliptical (egg-shaped) rather than circular; that the planets do not travel at constant speeds; and that the closer a planet is to the Sun the faster it moves. Kepler's Three Laws helped prove Copernicus's theory because they explained planetary movements that had puzzled people since ancient times. One thing puzzled Kepler, though. What kept the planets moving around the Sun instead of flying out into space? Kepler concluded that the Sun shot out some kind of mysterious rays that held the planets in orbit.

In 1608, the year before Kepler described the planets' motions in his book *New Astronomy*, an eyeglass maker in the Netherlands revolutionized astronomy. Hans Lippershey attached lenses to the oppo-

Galileo Galilei (1564–1642), the first astronomer to make astronomical discoveries with a telescope.

site ends of a tube and created the first telescope. Galileo Galilei soon became the first astronomer to observe the heavens with a telescope. Born in Pisa, Italy, in 1564, Galileo was a man of many achievements. He invented the thermometer. In experiments said to have taken place at the Leaning Tower of Pisa, he discovered that light objects fall as quickly as heavy objects. Utilizing Lippershey's techniques, Galileo built his first telescope in 1609 and soon beheld many astonishing sights.

Often, at night, a white cloudy patch can be seen stretching across the sky. American Indians believed that it was the path dead souls followed to heaven. The ancient Greeks thought that it resembled spilled milk, which is why it became known as the Milky Way. When Galileo aimed his telescope at the Milky Way, he discovered that it is composed of stars "so numerous as to be almost beyond belief." When he gazed at the Moon, he learned that it has mountains and craters. Galileo also discovered that Venus undergoes phases like the Moon, and that Saturn has what looked to him like handles on its sides. Galileo's telescope lacked the power to show that these "handles" were actually Saturn's rings, but it was strong enough to reveal something startling about Jupiter. Observing the giant planet night after night in January of 1610, Galileo saw that it was orbited by four moons. Here was absolute proof that Ptolemy had been wrong when he claimed that every heavenly body circled the Earth.

What he had seen with his own eyes helped make Galileo a staunch defender of the Copernican System. He described his observations in a booklet entitled *Messenger of the Stars* and built more telescopes, which he sold throughout Europe. Many people who read Galileo's booklet or viewed Jupiter's moons through his telescopes became convinced that the Earth could not be the center of the Universe.

Galileo's writings disturbed Church officials far more than those of Johannes Kepler, whose Three Laws involved difficult mathematics

Galileo (at right of telescope) showing people the moons of Jupiter orbiting the giant planet.

that few people understood. Anyone could understand Galileo's descriptions of Jupiter's moons, or even see them by peeking through a telescope. Religious leaders claimed that the telescopic images were the Devil's work, and in 1616 warned Galileo to stop supporting the Copernican System.

Galileo evaded the Church's order in an ingenious way. For five years he worked on a book entitled *Dialogue Concerning the Two Chief Systems of the World*, which was published in 1632, when he was sixty-eight years old. So that less-educated people could read it, Galileo wrote *Dialogue* in Italian rather than in Latin, which was the language of scholars. And read it people did—by the thousands. The book concerns three friends who debate whether the Sun revolves around an unmoving Earth, as Ptolemy claimed, or the Earth spins and orbits the Sun, as Copernicus asserted. The author pretended to remain neutral, but it was clear that he favored the Copernican System. Readers admired Galileo's cleverness and marveled at his courage, for many of them remembered what had happened to Giordano Bruno for presenting similar ideas.

Church officials were not fooled by Galileo's literary technique. Galileo was arrested and brought before officials in Rome in 1633. The elderly scientist was commanded to get down on his knees and say that the Copernican System was false. Realizing that his life hung in the balance, Galileo obeyed the order. Denying the truth saved his life, which was fortunate for science. He was imprisoned in his own home, where he spent his last years studying motion and pondering the question: Why do objects fall to Earth?

The man who would answer that question was born in Woolsthorpe, England, on Christmas Day of 1642—the year Galileo died. Isaac Newton left school at fourteen to help run the family farm, but he was far more interested in science than in tending sheep. Young Isaac built a little windmill that was powered by a pet mouse. He also liked to tie a lantern to a kite, which he flew on dark nights, convincing his neighbors that a new comet had appeared in the sky. His absentmindedness became legendary. It was claimed that when he was pondering a scientific problem, Isaac sometimes forgot to eat or put on his clothes.

Realizing that Isaac was not suited for farming, his mother sent him to study science and mathematics at Cambridge University. He graduated in 1665 and was about to begin teaching at Cambridge when the school closed due to an epidemic. Twenty-two-year-old Newton returned to his family farm. There, within a year and a half, he had invented a new type of telescope and made three of the greatest discoveries in the history of science.

The earliest telescopes, called *refractors*, all worked with lenses. Newton's invention, called the *reflecting telescope* or the *Newtonian reflector*, worked with mirrors and could be built of much greater size and power than refracting telescopes. (Today the world's largest optical telescopes are all reflectors.) Newton's interest in telescopes helped involve him in the study of color and light. Using a triangular piece of glass called a *prism*, he discovered that light is composed of a variety of blended colors. Sunlight, for example, proved to be a rainbow of colors when passed through his prism. Newton named the bands of color that make up light the *spectrum*—Latin for "ghost." Thanks to Newton's discovery, astronomers learned to determine the chemical composition, temperature, and motion of heavenly bodies by studying their spectrums. Newton's second discovery, the branch of mathematics called calculus, is also of great help to astronomers. But it was his third discovery during his year and a half at home that became his most famous achievement.

Newton believed in the Copernican System, but, like Kepler and Galileo, he wondered why objects fall to Earth and why the planets keep moving around the Sun instead of flying out into space. One

afternoon in the autumn of 1666, Newton was sitting in an orchard when an apple fell from a tree. He suddenly realized that the same force that pulled the apple to the ground also keeps the planets in orbit around the Sun and the Moon in orbit around the Earth. This force became known as *gravitation* or *gravity* from the Latin word *gravis*, meaning "heavy." In his famous book *Mathematical Principles*, which was published in 1687, Newton explained how gravitation and motion make the Copernican Universe work.

Although no single moment marked the triumph of the Copernican System, *Mathematical Principles* ended all serious objections to it. Thanks to Newton, Copernicus, and a number of others who had "stood upon the shoulders of giants," by the year 1700 most of the world realized that a sixth planet had been added to the five known since antiquity—the one we call Earth. (Figure 5)

Opposite page: Isaac Newton
(1642–1727) analyzing sunlight.
Newton discovered that light is made
up of bands of color, which he called
the "spectrum."

◗ THREE ◗

Planet Number Seven: Uranus

While I was examining the small stars in the neighbourhood of H Geminorum, I perceived [an object] that appeared visibly larger than the rest.

William Herschel, discoverer of Uranus

✸ By 1781 astronomy books listed six planets: Mercury, Venus, Earth, Mars, Jupiter, and Saturn. (Figures 6–11) Actually, a seventh major body orbiting the Sun had been sighted numerous times, but no one had recognized it as a planet.

The planets lie in the Zodiac, a belt of twelve constellations that encircles the sky. A person with sharp vision who knows where to look in the Zodiac at a given time may locate what appears to be a dim greenish star. A small telescope reveals that the object is not a star, for it shines with a steady light instead of twinkling. Also, stars are so distant that they remain points of light even under high magnification, while this object enlarges into a tiny ball when seen through a telescope. This body is the seventh planet from the Sun: Uranus.

Ancient people did not know about Uranus, for although barely visible to the naked eye, it isn't bright enough to be identified as a planet without a telescope. Yet even after the telescope was invented, Uranus was viewed time after time without anyone realizing what it was. The first astronomer known to have seen the seventh planet without knowing it was John Flamsteed of England, in 1690. From drawings and descriptions by other astronomers, we know that the object was viewed through telescopes more than twenty other times over the next ninety-one years without being recognized as a planet. Perhaps in some cases the viewers' telescopes were too weak to show the planetary disk. Other observers mistook the object for a comet—a body that develops a long glowing tail when near the Sun but that resembles a planet when far away. Still other astronomers did not study the object with enough care. The failure of earlier scientists to make the discovery proved to be a later man's gain.

Friedrich Wilhelm Herschel was born in Hanover, Germany, in 1738. Wilhelm, as he was called, had three brothers and two sisters, including Caroline, who was twelve years his junior. Wilhelm's father, who played the oboe in the Hanoverian Guards military band, taught his children music. One of Wilhelm's first memories was of being placed on a table at the age of four to play a miniature violin his father had made. Mr. Herschel also took his children outside at night to show them the constellations and talk to them about astronomy. Wilhelm and his brothers all slept in one bed. In her memoirs, Caroline recalled that at night Wilhelm would chatter away about astronomy to his brothers, only to find that his talking had put them to sleep.

When he was fourteen, Wilhelm joined his father's band as an oboist and violinist. Several years later, Germany entered the Seven Years' War, which involved most of the nations of Europe. The band went off to provide marching music for the soldiers, which was how Wilhelm found himself in the midst of a major battle near Hanover in 1757. "We were so near the field of action as to be within reach of the gunshots," he wrote in his diary. As he fled with the remnants of his unit, Wilhelm decided that the military life was not for him. Later that year he obtained a discharge and moved to England.

In his adopted country, Wilhelm changed his name to William Herschel and went to work as a musician. He bought a horse and often traveled more than fifty miles a day from town to town to perform in concerts. Once when stranded without money, William gave a one-man concert, playing two horns and a harp, with one of the horns strapped to his shoulder. In his free time he wrote music, for his ambition was to become a great composer. Finally, in 1766, he won a steady job as a church choir director and organist in the city of Bath, England. William also became a popular music teacher and was soon giving forty private lessons a week in addition to his church duties. In 1772 he returned to Germany to ask his sister Caroline to come live with him. Caroline, who sang and played the harpsichord, moved into William's house, forming a musical and scientific partnership with him that would last for fifty years.

When Caroline joined him in Bath, William was becoming highly interested in mathematics, which he thought would improve his musical harmony. So closely are music, mathematics, and astronomy related that the ancient Greeks believed the planets vibrate in a mathematical harmony known as the "music of the spheres." Herschel's mathematical studies led him to adopt astronomy as a hobby, and around 1773 he bought a telescope.

William Herschel enjoyed stargazing so much that he decided to build larger telescopes than those he could buy. He and Caroline turned their house into a combination music school–telescope factory–observatory. For about twelve hours each day, the Herschels taught music. Between lessons and in their spare time, they made telescopes. William, who once commented that he became "sick when idle—it kills me almost to do nothing," was known to work at telescope building for twenty-four hours at a time! On clear nights, William and Caroline used their telescopes to study the heavens. One of them (usually William) would look through the telescope while the other (usually Caroline) made notes. Were it not for cloudy nights, Caroline remarked, she and her brother might have never slept. When William was too preoccupied to stop to eat, Caroline would place bits of food in his mouth as he worked. When he was at a task that required no concentration, she would read to him. In return, at a time when women generally received little education, William gave his sister lessons in astronomy and advanced mathematics.

William Herschel (1738–1822) and his sister Caroline Herschel (1750–1848) working at their telescope.

Astronomy soon replaced music as William Herschel's greatest interest. It was good that it did, for, in the opinion of music experts, he had little talent as a composer. But as an astronomer, William had no equal.

Around 1779, he assigned himself a stupendous task. He would make "reviews" of the whole sky, meaning that he would view *every* heavenly body visible through his telescope. This was akin to reading every book in a library; but most libraries have thousands of books while Herschel's telescope could reveal many millions of stars. Figuring that it would require six hundred years to study the sky in as much detail as he wanted,

Herschel decided to do the next best thing and make two kinds of observations. He would sweep his telescope across large areas of the sky in search of objects that merited closer study, and he would examine selected spots in detail. His goal was to gain what he called "a knowledge of the construction of the heavens." William Herschel relished the enormous challenge of trying to understand the basic structure of the Universe. "This will be a work of some years," he wrote to a friend. "But it is, to me, so far from laborious, that it is attended with the utmost delight." The project actually spanned several decades, but, true to his word, Herschel never lost his delight in the work.

One night in March of 1781, while engaged in the second of the four all-sky investigations he made during his lifetime, William Herschel noticed an odd object in the region of the constellation Gemini the Twins. Of this object he wrote:

> *On Tuesday the 13th March, between ten and eleven in the evening, while I was examining the small stars in the neighbourhood of H Geminorum, I perceived one that appeared visibly larger than the rest; being struck with its uncommon magnitude, I compared it to H Geminorum and the small star in the quartile between Auriga and Gemini, and finding it so much larger than either of them, suspected it to be a comet.*

Far more interested in the distant stars than in the relatively nearby objects in the Solar System, Herschel at first felt little excitement about the "suspected comet." However, he did something that later entitled him to be hailed as the discoverer of a new planet. He wrote a paper entitled "Account of a Comet," which he sent to the Royal Society of London. Based on Herschel's written description of its position, the object was located by other astronomers. They concluded that it was not a comet but a previously unknown planet about twice as far from the Sun as Saturn.

For alerting the world to the object, William Herschel was hailed as the first discoverer of a planet (besides Earth) since prehistoric people spotted Mercury, Venus, Mars, Jupiter, and Saturn. He also became the target of a great deal of jealousy. Unlike most astronomers, he had not attended Cambridge or Oxford in England or any of the other leading European universities. In fact, he hadn't gone to college at all. Moreover, he was an amateur astronomer who still earned his living through music. Deeply resentful of this upstart who was suddenly so famous, some professional astronomers claimed that his discovery of the planet was merely a matter of luck. Herschel, who was described

William Herschel

as an "openly happy and gentle" man by people who knew him, politely pointed out that his finding the planet was due to hard work. "It has generally been supposed that a lucky accident brought this [planet] to my view," he wrote. "This is a mistake. In the regular manner that I examined every star in the heavens . . . it was that night *its turn* to be discovered."

As astronomers computed the new planet's orbit, the public had a practical concern: What should it be named? The discovery had occurred at a sad moment in English history. In the fall of 1781, George Washington's forces won America's independence from England, transforming the Thirteen Colonies into the United States of America. People in England lamented that King George III had "lost the jewels in his crown." William Herschel offered to replace the colonies with a jewel in the sky. He suggested that the new planet be named *Georgium Sidus*—"George's Star" in Latin. This would forever commemorate the fact that the planet had been discovered in England when George III was king.

For about seventy years, some English people followed Herschel's suggestion and called the planet "Georgium Sidus," "the Georgian Planet," or simply "the Georgian." None of these names became popular outside of England, however. For one thing, they weren't "catchy." Second, the object was a planet, not a star. Third, the king had not contributed to the discovery. And fourth, non-English people, particularly the Americans who had just fought a war against his forces, had no desire to honor George III.

People in France felt that the planet should be named for its discoverer, and began calling it "Herschel's Planet" or "Herschel." Neither name went into widespread use. The same was true of "Dumbbell," a suggestion that was made because the planet had made fools of astronomers by remaining undiscovered for so long.

Most astronomers favored a name from ancient mythology. Two that were proposed unsuccessfully were *Hypercronius*, meaning "beyond Saturn," and *Cybele*, for the wife of Saturn. Johann Elert Bode, a German astronomer, thought that the planet should be named *Uranus* (Figure 12) for the Greek and Roman god of the sky. Bode's suggestion seemed fitting, for it maintained the family relationship in the planetary names. Jupiter was the father of Mercury, Venus, and Mars. Saturn was Jupiter's father. Uranus (also known as Father Sky) and Gaea (also known as Mother Earth) were Saturn's parents. The name Uranus triumphed in most of the world and was eventually adopted in England, too.

William and Caroline Herschel went on to have remarkable careers. King George III hired them to be the royal family's personal astronomers. One night the princesses (King George and Queen Charlotte had nine sons and six daughters) wanted to stargaze, but the sky was cloudy. William created an artificial Saturn out of pasteboard, attached it to a wall, and then showed it to the princesses through his telescope.

Thanks partly to the king's support, the Herschels made many more discoveries. Caroline, who is remembered as the first professional woman astronomer, made comet hunting her specialty. Before she died at the age of ninety-eight, Caroline Herschel

Caroline Herschel

discovered eight comets. In 1789, William built a telescope with a forty-foot-long tube and a forty-eight-inch-diameter mirror. For many years this massive instrument was the world's largest telescope and considered one of the wonders of the modern world. William Herschel used his telescopes to "look further into space than ever human being did before," as he told a friend. Among his achievements, he discovered two moons of Uranus and two of Saturn, and also correctly concluded that many of the blobs of light he saw through his telescopes were "Milky Ways," meaning huge star systems. In addition, he discovered infrared rays, which cannot be seen by the human eye but which are emitted as an object is heated.

William Herschel considered his discovery of Uranus a minor accomplishment compared to his research on "the construction of the heavens." Yet today much of his other work is forgotten and he is best remembered for locating the seventh planet from the Sun. Interestingly, Herschel lived to the age of eighty-four, the same number of years Uranus takes to orbit the Sun, so that at his death the planet he discovered had returned to almost the same exact spot in the sky where it had been at his birth.

FOUR

THE ASTEROIDS, OR MINOR PLANETS

*I have announced this object as a comet. But since it has no tail and, fur-
ther, since its movement is slow and rather uniform, it has occurred to me
several times that it might be something better than a comet.*

Giuseppe Piazzi, discoverer of Ceres, the first known asteroid

✸ In about 1765, a curious fact was discovered about the Solar
System. Each planet is roughly one and a half times the distance from
the Sun as the previous planet. For example, Earth is 93 million miles
from the Sun—approximately one and a half times as far as Venus,
which orbits our star at a distance of 67 million miles. Johann Elert
Bode, the man who named Uranus, popularized this mathematical
relationship of the planets' distances, and so it is called Bode's Law. To
this day, astronomers do not know why it holds true.

Astronomers of the late 1700s were puzzled by one place in the
Solar System where the formula didn't seem to work. Jupiter, at a distance of 484 million miles, is three times as far from the Sun as Mars.
Why were the two planets much farther apart than they ought to be
according to Bode's Law?

One possibility was that an undiscovered planet occupied the vast
empty space. Most astronomers scoffed at this idea. They pointed out

that Mars and Jupiter are both among the brightest objects in the night sky, which made it unlikely that a planet located between them could elude the naked eye, let alone the telescope. Some astronomers, however, believed that a small and/or dim planet could have been overlooked.

A group of six astronomers decided to search for a planet between Mars and Jupiter. In the fall of 1800, they met in Lilienthal, Germany, just ten miles from William Herschel's birthplace. The six men decided to divide the sky into twenty-four zones along the Zodiac and assign these regions to themselves and various other European planet hunters. Franz Xaver von Zach, one of the six founders, named the group the Lilienthal Detectives because they were searching for a missing planet. Because they were patrolling the sky, they were also known as the Celestial Police.

Meanwhile, in Palermo, Italy, astronomer Giuseppe Piazzi was working on a project worthy of William Herschel. A priest who was also director of Palermo Observatory, Piazzi had spent ten years compiling a catalog in which he listed the precise positions of thousands of stars. At the close of the first day of the nineteenth century—January 1, 1801—Piazzi was looking through his telescope as usual when he spied a faint object in the constellation Taurus the Bull that was not listed on his star maps. Observing the object on subsequent nights, Piazzi noted that it slowly wandered in relation to the background stars, which proved that it was a member of the Solar System. Like Herschel had done with Uranus, Piazzi at first concluded that he had found a comet. As he continued to track the mystery object, however, he realized that it didn't look or move like a comet. In a letter to a friend, he confessed his secret hope that "it might be something better than a comet," meaning a planet.

Opposite page:

Giuseppe Piazzi

(1746–1826)

Unfortunately, Piazzi became ill in mid-February and had to suspend his observations. By the time he recovered, the object had

moved too near a position in line with the Sun to be seen in the night sky. Piazzi spread the news about his discovery to other astronomers, but none of them, including William Herschel, could locate the object even after it emerged from the Sun's glare. Whatever Piazzi had found seemed to have disappeared—until the very last day of the year.

Karl Gauss, a twenty-four-year-old German mathematician, had read Piazzi's description of the unknown object. Using information supplied by Piazzi, Gauss tried to compute the position of what he called "that mite of a planet which has been lost to sight for nearly a year among the innumerable little stars of heaven." Gauss was not an observer of the skies, so he sent his calculations to someone who was—Franz Xaver von Zach of the Celestial Police. On December 31, 1801, von Zach spotted the object at nearly the exact spot in the sky where young Karl Gauss said it should be. The body that Giuseppe Piazzi had discovered with assists from Karl Gauss and Franz Xaver von Zach was determined to be located between Mars and Jupiter, and seemed to be the missing planet predicted by Bode's Law. Piazzi named the object *Ceres*, for Saturn's daughter, the Roman goddess of grain and the harvest.

Astronomers soon learned that Ceres wasn't like any other planet. To start with, it was much smaller. With a diameter of only 600 miles, Ceres could fit inside Jupiter, the largest planet, about three and a half million times. If we made a model of the Solar System in which Jupiter is represented by a tennis ball, Ceres would be the size of a grain of sand. Also, two more founders of the Celestial Police made the surprising discovery that Ceres wasn't the only miniature world located between Mars and Jupiter. In March of 1802, Heinrich Wilhelm Olbers discovered an object he named Pallas, which was smaller than Ceres. In 1804, Karl Harding found Juno, and in 1807 Olbers discovered Vesta. That seemed to be the last of the dwarf plan-ets, so in 1815 the Celestial Police ended their planet hunt. Later it was found that thousands of bodies even smaller than Ceres, Pallas, Vesta, and Juno lie between Mars and Jupiter. Most have odd shapes and are no bigger than a hill. Some are the size of a football.

These objects between Mars and Jupiter were similar to planets, astronomers realized, except that they were much smaller. Giuseppe Piazzi named them *planetoids*, meaning "resembling planets" or "planet like." That name is still occasionally used, as is the term *minor planets*, but another name that was briefly used has been discarded. The suffix *-kins* is sometimes placed on the end of a word to indicate smallness (as in munchkins or babykins), so a few people wanted to call the little objects *planetkins*. However, William Herschel coined the name by which they are most commonly known. "I shall call them *asteroids*," Herschel wrote in a paper on Ceres and Pallas that was published in 1802. Meaning "resembling stars" or "starlike," the name probably isn't as appropriate as planetoids, minor planets, or even planetkins. The objects do look like dim stars in telescopes, though, so the name stuck. (Figure 13)

The asteroids are believed to have been formed during the creation of the Solar System, about 4.6 billion years ago. Some astronomers say that they are pieces of the early Solar System that failed to come together to form a planet. Others think that they are the remains of a planet that collided with another heavenly body and then broke apart. Several asteroids have unusual orbits that take them close to Earth. In 1996 a small asteroid known as JA$_1$ approached to within 280,000 miles of our planet (a little more than the distance between Earth and the Moon)—one of the nearest misses on record. As will be discussed later, comets or asteroids that slammed into the Earth in the distant past may have changed the course of our planet's natural history.

FIVE

THE EIGHTH PLANET: NEPTUNE

[I] formed a design, in the beginning of this week, of investigating, as soon as possible after taking my degree, the irregularities in the motion of Uranus . . . in order to find whether they may be attributed to the action of an undiscovered planet beyond it.

John Couch Adams, co-discoverer of Neptune

✳ Soon after William Herschel discovered Uranus in 1781, the planet was found to wander away from the orbit it was expected to follow according to Newton's Laws of Gravitation. Bewildered by the seventh planet's wobbles, a few astronomers questioned whether gravity always worked as Newton described in the Solar System's outer regions. Most held the more sensible opinion that Uranus was being disturbed by the gravitational pull of an undiscovered eighth planet.

Actually, the planet had already been seen without being recognized, as had occurred with Uranus. Notes and drawings made by Galileo show that he observed Neptune on December 28, 1612— *234 years* before its official discovery. Had Galileo's telescope been powerful enough to distinguish it from the stars, the eighth planet might have been discovered before the seventh planet! Records left by French astronomer Joseph Lalande indictate that he observed

Neptune on May 8 and 10, 1795, but he did not identify it as a planet either. As a result, by 1840 astronomers were scanning the skies in search of an undiscovered planet beyond Uranus.

Ever since the age of Tycho Brahe and Johannes Kepler, there have been two kinds of astronomers. Some, like Brahe, prefer to observe the sky, while others, like Kepler, would rather form theories and compute orbits. John Couch Adams belonged to the latter group. Born into a farming family in Cornwall, England, in 1819, John displayed his mathematical genius as a child. By the time he was twelve years old he was performing difficult calculus problems and reading every astronomy book he could find. A few years later, his family enrolled him at Cambridge—the university Isaac Newton had attended. One day while in a Cambridge bookstore, Adams picked up a work about Uranus's unusual movements by the English astronomer George Airy. Adams told a classmate: "Uranus is a long way out of his course. I mean to find out why. I think I know." He made a note to himself that upon graduation, he would study "the irregularities in the motion of Uranus . . . in order to find whether they may be attributed to the action of an undiscovered planet beyond it."

Following his graduation in 1843, Adams began computing the unknown planet's position by analyzing the orbit of Uranus. The problem involved such complex mathematics that George Airy, whose writings had inspired Adams, claimed that determining the eighth planet's position would require centuries. With the help of Bode's Law, John Couch Adams completed his calculations in just two years, arriving at his answer by September of 1845, when he was only twenty-six years old. His conclusion was so close to the planet's actual location that, had he owned a small telescope, Adams could have found the planet himself rather easily. He did not have access to a telescope, however, so he needed to convince someone who did to conduct a search.

Adams contacted James Challis, director of Cambridge

Observatory, in the hope that he would attempt the planet hunt. Had Challis aimed his observatory's large telescope where Adams advised, he might be remembered today as the co-discoverer of Neptune. Unfortunately, Challis had so little confidence in the young man's calculations that he decided to get rid of him by sending him to George Airy, who held England's leading astronomical post—Astronomer Royal at Greenwich Observatory outside of London. The only help Challis provided Adams was a letter of introduction that he wrote to Airy for him:

> *My friend Mr. Adams (who will probably deliver this note to you) has completed his calculations regarding the perturbation of Uranus by a supposed ulterior planet, and has arrived at results which he would be glad to communicate to you personally, if you could spare him a few moments of your valuable time.*

Expecting that the Astronomer Royal would be pleased to learn that he had inspired him to solve what Airy had called a "nearly impossible" problem, Adams eagerly set out for Greenwich. He arrived at the observatory in late September of 1845, only to find that Dr. Airy was at a meeting in France. Adams left his letter of introduction and said that he would return in about a month. When he did so, Adams found that Airy was at a meeting in London but was expected momentarily. The young mathematician left his card with Mrs. Airy, along with a brief paper describing his results, and said that he would come back in an hour.

Sixty minutes later, John Couch Adams again knocked on the door and informed the butler that he had an important matter to discuss with Dr. Airy. The Astronomer Royal was at dinner and refused to be disturbed, the butler responded. As he left Greenwich Observatory,

Opposite page:
John Couch
Adams
(1819–1892)

Adams felt crushed. He had hoped that Airy would study his calculations and ask him to join in the planet hunt with one of the observatory's telescopes. Instead, after two years of work on the problem, Adams couldn't even speak to the Astronomer Royal.

Besides being impolite, George Airy's snub of Adams proved to be one of the biggest blunders in the history of astronomy. A Galileo or a Herschel would have leaped at the chance to find a new planet, but Airy had two huge faults as a scientist. He lacked curiosity, preferring to study the known planets rather than look for new ones, and he was hostile to any work that wasn't his own. The Astronomer Royal also had serious flaws as a person. He seemed to be indifferent to other people's feelings, and he was snobbish. Airy had little respect for Adams because he was unknown, the son of poor farmers, and only half his age. Poor, foolish George Airy! Had he been able to gaze into the future, he might have rushed out after Adams, for in refusing to meet with the young man, he missed the great opportunity of his life.

Although he would not speak to Adams in person, Airy did read the short paper the young man had dropped off. The Astronomer Royal wrote Adams a note expressing disdain for his work and explaining that a search for the planet was not worth the time and effort of Greenwich Observatory. Still, Airy must have suspected that there was something to the calculations, for he showed Adams's short paper to Reverend William Dawes, an amateur astronomer. Adams's miserable luck continued. Dawes wanted to search for the planet, but he was busy building an observatory, so he passed Adams's calculations on to William Lassell, a brewer in Liverpool, England, who had built one of the largest telescopes of his time. Six years later, in 1851, Lassell would discover two moons of Uranus, but in the fall of 1845 he couldn't engage in a planet hunt, for he was in bed resting a badly injured ankle. By the time Lassell was up and about, he couldn't find Dawes's letter describing Adams's results. It is said that Lassell's maid accidentally threw the letter in the trash!

At the time that John Couch Adams was determining the position of the eighth planet, a French scientist was doing the same thing. Urbain Leverrier had much in common with Adams. He was born in 1811 in France's Normandy region, just across the English Channel from Adams's home county of Cornwall, England. Like Adams, Leverrier came from a rather poor but tight-knit family. The Leverriers sold their house to send Urbain to college. He rewarded them by earning the highest honors at the university in Paris. Leverrier became a chemist, but he had a gift for mathematics, so in his mid-twenties he turned to astronomy. His specialty was calculating orbits. In the summer of 1845, Leverrier began researching the unusual motions of Uranus. A year later, in June of 1846, he presented his results to the French Academy of Sciences. An eighth planet was pulling at Uranus, he asserted, and he knew its location. His conclusions were close to those of Adams, who by this time had been waiting nine months for someone to aim a telescope at the place he suggested.

Leverrier suffered the same disappointment that Adams did. No one in France seemed to take his calculations seriously. Incredibly, the person who finally took notice was George Airy! Leverrier's paper circulated in England, and when Airy read it he realized that ignoring Adams had been a serious mistake. Leverrier's prediction agreed with Adams's to within half a degree of the sky. The sky is divided into 180 degrees from horizon to horizon, so a half-degree difference was too close to be a coincidence. The likeliest explanation was that both men were on target in computing the eighth planet's position.

Astronomers are often portrayed as absentminded people who are beyond petty disputes and ambitions because they have their "heads in the stars." The truth is that most astronomers have as much professional jealousy and competitiveness as anyone else. As he studied

Leverrier's paper, George Airy had a very down-to-earth worry. England and France had been fierce rivals for centuries. How would it look if Airy found the eighth planet based on a Frenchman's calculations, and then it was revealed that he had ignored an Englishman who had reached the same conclusion nearly a year earlier? Airy was in the odd position for a scientist of *not* wanting to take part in a discovery. Instead, his goal was to protect his reputation.

Airy had an additional problem. William Herschel's son John Herschel, himself a noted astronomer on the Greenwich Observatory Board, wanted Airy to find the object that was disturbing the planet his father had discovered sixty-five years earlier. Seeing that he had to do something, Airy decided to hand the problem back to James Challis, who had gotten him into this fix by sending Adams to him in the first place. On July 9, 1846, Airy wrote Challis a letter that began: "You know that I attach importance to the examination of that part of the heavens in which there is . . . reason for suspecting the existence of a planet exterior to Uranus." Four days later, Airy advised Challis to "sweep [the Zodiac] for the possible planet" rather than search where Adams and Leverrier advised.

Sweeps had been appropriate for William Herschel, because he couldn't study every object in the sky in detail, but in this case they were a waste of time, because two astronomers had indicated where to look for the eighth planet. Perhaps Airy secretly hoped that Challis wouldn't find the planet, and that a Frenchman would spot it first. That way the French were likely to gain all the credit for the discovery, and Airy's neglect of Adams might be overlooked. Airy then planned a long European trip—probably praying that the French would find the planet in his absence and the whole mess would blow over.

Meanwhile, Urbain Leverrier was disgusted at the lack of enthusiasm over his work in his own country, and finally decided to seek help elsewhere. Months earlier Johann Galle, an astronomer at Germany's

Opposite page:

Urbain Leverrier

(1811–1877)

Berlin Observatory, had sent Leverrier a paper he had written. In September of 1846 Leverrier wrote back to Galle praising his paper. He also enclosed his prediction for the location of the eighth planet and politely requested that Galle search for it.

Galle received the letter on September 23 and asked observatory director Johann Encke if he could use the big refracting telescope that night. Encke gave his permission, for he was celebrating his birthday that evening and wasn't planning to work. Heinrich d'Arrest, a college student employed by the observatory, overheard the conversation and asked to help Galle in the planet search. After the Sun went down on September 23, 1846, Johann Galle and Heinrich d'Arrest opened the Berlin Observatory dome and aimed the telescope at the place near the boundary of the constellations Aquarius the Water Bearer and Capricorn the Goat, where Leverrier claimed the planet was located.

As Galle looked through the telescope eyepiece, d'Arrest studied a map of the stars of the region. Each time Galle saw a star, he called out its position and brightness. D'Arrest then found it on the star map and called out, "On the chart." Over the next few minutes, Galle described one star after another and d'Arrest said "On the chart" again and again. They had been searching for less than an hour when Galle spied a greenish-blue object. After Galle described it, d'Arrest excitedly answered: "That object is not on the chart!"

The two astronomers hoped that the object was not on the map because it was a planet orbiting the Sun and therefore changed position over time relative to the stars. Galle and d'Arrest pulled Encke away from his birthday party. For several hours, Encke observed the object with them. The three men suspected that they were viewing the eighth planet, but they weren't certain that the object had a planetary disk, and one night wasn't long enough to determine if it appeared to move among the stars.

The sky above Berlin Observatory remained clear the next night, so once again the three astronomers focused their telescope on the unknown object. They immediately saw that it had moved slightly in relation to the stars. Not only that, but this time they were positive that, unlike a star, the object appeared as a small disk or ball. The hunt for the eighth planet had ended.

The next day Galle sent Leverrier a congratulatory letter. "The planet whose position you have pointed out actually exists," he wrote. "The same day that I received your letter, I found a star of the eighth magnitude which was not on our chart. . . . The observations made the next night determined that this was the sought-for planet." Encke, too, sent Leverrier a note praising his "brilliant discovery." To other astronomers, though, Encke sent out word that he and Galle had found the planet, without mentioning that d'Arrest had actually assisted Galle.

Within a few days, newspapers throughout Europe announced that Berlin Observatory had found the eighth planet based on Urbain Leverrier's calculations. John Couch Adams wasn't a resentful kind of person, but as he read the articles praising Leverrier, he felt a trace of bitterness. He had predicted the planet's location nearly a year before Leverrier. If only George Airy or James Challis had acted on his information, Adams would have been hailed as the discoverer.

When Challis read about the discovery, he went back and checked his observational records. He found that not taking Adams seriously hadn't been his only mistake. While sweeping the sky in search of the planet, Challis had spotted it at least twice in August—several weeks before it was identified in Berlin. The problem was, Challis had not recognized the object for what it was. "The planet was in my grasp," Challis later wrote to Airy, "if only I had examined or mapped the observations."

As he had planned, Airy was still away on his trip when the new planet was discovered. Because several astronomers knew that he had ignored Adams, Airy figured his best strategy was to make Adams's work seem unimportant compared to Leverrier's. Airy wrote to Leverrier, declaring: "You are to be recognized beyond doubt as the real predictor of the planet's place. I may add that the English investigations, as I believe, were not quite so extensive as yours." But Airy's plot was foiled, for a famous English astronomer would not let John Couch Adams be pushed into the background.

On October 3, ten days after the planet's discovery, an article about Adams's work by John Herschel appeared in a London magazine. Herschel explained: "A conclusion as to the situation of a new planet very nearly coincident with Leverrier's [was] arrived at, in entire ignorance of [Leverrier's calculations], by a young Cambridge mathematician, Mr. Adams—who will, I hope, pardon this mention of his name (the matter being one of great historical moment)—and who will, doubtless, in his own good time and manner, place his calculations before the public."

Herschel's article enraged the French. England had often seized land on Earth claimed by France. Now the English seemed to be trying to steal an entire planet! Leverrier angrily asked why Airy and Challis hadn't mentioned Adams's work in their congratulatory letters to him. French newspapers attacked the English astronomers Airy, Challis, Adams, and Herschel, as well as the British people in general.

Instead of fighting for credit, John Couch Adams poured his energy into computing the new planet's orbit and size. On November 13, at a meeting of England's Royal Astronomical Society, Adams presented a paper in which he explained what he had learned about the eighth planet, pointing out that he had predicted its position before Leverrier. At the same time, Adams made it clear that he did not want to battle over the glory. "I mention these dates to show that my results were arrived at independently and previously to the publication of Leverrier, and not with the intention of interfering with his just claims to the honors of the discovery," said Adams, "for there is no doubt that his researches . . . led to the actual discovery of the planet by Dr. Galle." Adams's modesty and graciousness won him a large following in England, where Airy and Challis were increasingly seen as the villains in the affair.

The events had been so confusing that it was not certain whom history would crown as the discoverer. The French favored Leverrier, whose work had led directly to locating the planet. People in Germany reminded everyone that Galle, d'Arrest, and Encke had been the first to recognize the planet in the sky. The English insisted that Adams had been the first to reveal the planet's position—even if it was only on paper. (Figure 14)

The public awaited another decision. What would the eighth planet be called? Johann Galle proposed "Janus," for the Roman god of doors, but few people liked that name. George Airy and James Challis favored "Oceanus," referring to the ocean, but no one would accept a name submitted by this pair, whose only contribution was to delay the discovery. John Couch Adams seems to have made no suggestion, but Urbain Leverrier made up for Adams's modesty by proposing two names. First he suggested that the planet be named "Neptune," for the Roman god of the sea. Within a few days, Leverrier formulated a new plan. The name of the planet Uranus should be changed to "Herschel," claimed Leverrier—the very name the French had proposed sixty-five years earlier. "In my future researches," Leverrier wrote, "I shall eliminate the name *Uranus* completely, and call the planet only by the name *Herschel*." Leverrier hoped the English would be so pleased by this suggestion that they wouldn't object if the eighth planet were named "Leverrier" for himself!

As Leverrier must have expected, the English ignored his second proposal. They were just becoming accustomed to the name "Uranus" instead of "the Georgian" for the seventh planet, and had no interest in switching to "Herschel"; besides, they did not want to be reminded of their missed opportunity by having the eighth planet named for a Frenchman. Leverrier's first choice struck most people as perfect, however, for Neptune was the son of Saturn, which kept the planetary names in the family of the ancient gods and goddesses. *Neptune* easily won out over all other contenders.

The question of who discovered Neptune has not been answered so easily. Because his calculations were ignored through no fault of his own, Adams today is generally considered the co-discoverer of Neptune with Leverrier. Many historians also credit Johann Galle, and sometimes Heinrich d'Arrest and Johann Encke, with contributing to the discovery. Yet, to this day, schoolchildren in different countries learn different versions of the story. For example, a French encyclopedia begins its article on the planet by saying: "NEPTUNE, a planet of the Solar System, the eighth planet from the Sun, was discovered in 1846 by Leverrier." On the other hand, children who open a German encyclopedia learn that: "Neptune, the eighth planet in the Solar System . . . was in the year 1846 discovered by J. G. Galle, although its existence was predicted by Leverrier."

There is an interesting footnote to the "Neptune controversy," as it is known. In June of 1847, John Herschel gave a party to which he invited both Adams and Leverrier. Some people feared that sparks would fly when the two main contestants for the discovery of Neptune first met. But Leverrier and Adams liked each other immediately and remained friends into old age as both men continued their successful scientific careers.

SIX

VULCAN: THE PHANTOM PLANET

There has not passed a single day [in the previous thirty years], without the Sun being examined, drawn, or photographed in Italy, England, Portugal, Spain, America, France, and elsewhere. That the supposed [intra-Mercurial] planet has never been seen means that it is either well hidden, or it does not exist.

French astronomer Camille Flammarion, writing in about 1890

✴ A few years after the discovery of Neptune, Urbain Leverrier became involved in one of the oddest episodes in the history of planet hunting. Ever since the 1700s, astronomers had realized that Mercury, the innermost known planet, did not precisely follow its predicted orbit. Something seemed to be tugging at the swift little planet, slightly altering its expected movement around the Sun.

Several possible explanations were put forth. One was that Mercury possessed an unseen moon that was pulling at it. Another was that a swarm of asteroids near the Sun was affecting Mercury's motion. A third theory was that an undiscovered planet nearer to the Sun than Mercury was disturbing the orbit of the hot orange sphere.

An obstacle to finding the "intra-Mercurial planet" (meaning the theoretical planet within the orbit of Mercury) was that the glare of the nearby Sun would make it difficult or even impossible to spot.

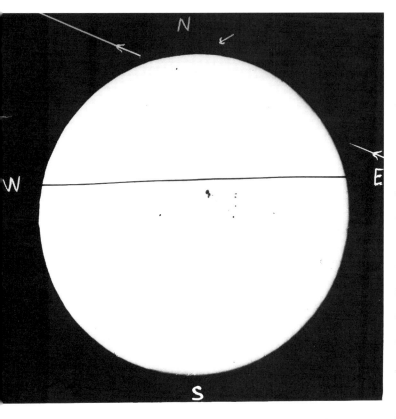

The arrows point to a little black speck under the *N*. That speck is Mercury in transit across the Sun, while the other markings are sunspots.

Still, there was a possible way to prove the planet's existence. Now and then Mercury and Venus cross in front of the Sun from our vantage point on Earth. During these *transits*, Mercury and Venus appear as round little balls silhouetted against the Sun. Since looking directly at the Sun with a telescope or just with the naked eye can damage a person's vision, astronomers observe transits of Mercury and Venus across the Sun with special devices. In the early 1800s, several astronomers began studying the Sun in the hope of seeing the intra-Mercurial planet when it crossed our star's disk. Heinrich Schwabe, an amateur astronomer in Germany, was one of the most persistent of these planet hunters.

Schwabe was a pharmacist. Since he worked nights preparing medicines, he realized that if he wanted to pursue astronomy, he had to find a way to do it by day. He began observing the Sun in 1826. Every clear day for nearly twenty years, Schwabe studied the Sun in the hope of seeing the intra-Mercurial planet. While doing so, he learned a great deal about sunspots—irregularly shaped dark areas on the Sun that are thought to be caused by magnetic disturbances. Sunspots create natural light displays in our night sky known as auroras, and they also seem to affect our weather in ways that we are just starting to understand. However, in all Schwabe's years of observing the Sun, no new planet ever moved into his view.

In 1847 Edward Herrick, an American astronomer, began hunting for the intra-Mercurial planet. He didn't find it, either, nor did several other planet hunters. Still, as Urban Leverrier phrased it, "some as yet unknown force" was disturbing Mercury. In September of 1859 Leverrier described Mercury's orbital abnormalities to the French Academy of Sciences in Paris. He told the academy that he thought an asteroid belt near Mercury was the likeliest cause, but that astronomers shouldn't give up the search for an undiscovered planet near the Sun.

On December 22, 1859, just a few weeks after Leverrier spoke to the academy, he received a letter from Edmund Lescarbault, a physician and amateur astronomer in the French village of Orgères, not far from Paris. Dr. Lescarbault claimed that on March 26 he had seen a small round body transit across the Sun. No transits of Mercury or Venus had occurred that day. If Lescarbault's observation was reliable, Urban Leverrier realized, the country doctor could have located the intra-Mercurial planet.

The famous French astronomer Camille Flammarion vouched for the doctor's honesty. Still, Leverrier felt, the most logical explanation was that Lescarbault's eyes had played tricks on him or that he had mistaken a sunspot for the silhouette of a passing planet.

On December 30, 1859, Leverrier visited Dr. Lescarbault. "So you are the man," Leverrier reportedly said, "who pretends to have seen an intra-Mercurial planet. Why did you wait nine months to write to me? Tell me at once truthfully what you have seen."

As Lescarbault described his observation, the co-discoverer of Neptune was impressed by the doctor's sincerity and astronomical knowledge. After an hour with Lescarbault, Urban Leverrier asked the townspeople about the doctor's character. Everyone he met said that Dr. Lescarbault was a man of integrity. Urbain Leverrier departed Orgères believing that a new planet had been discovered. He chose an appropriate name for a planet near the Sun—Vulcan, for the Roman god of fire. Dr. Lescarbault was viewed as another Johann Galle, the man who had found Neptune based on Leverrier's calculations, and was presented with France's highest award, the Legion of Honor, by Emperor Napoleon III. Although Leverrier hadn't done much except say that the object might exist, he was hailed as the predictor of both the innermost (Vulcan) and the outermost (Neptune) known planets of the time.

Urbain Leverrier did some research and uncovered what he believed were several earlier observations of Vulcan. Based on these and Lescarbault's observations, Leverrier calculated Vulcan's orbit. His results were exciting. Vulcan, it was predicted, would again transit the Sun on March 29, April 2, and April 7, 1860.

Astronomers around the world eagerly aimed their telescopes at the Sun on those three days. They saw sunspots as usual, but no planetary silhouette passed in front of the Sun. It was possible that the orbital calculations were slightly off, and that Vulcan would transit the Sun later than predicted, so astronomers continued to look, day after day, year after year.

They never saw Vulcan because it didn't exist.

There are several possibilities about what Dr. Lescarbault had witnessed. Perhaps he was the victim of an optical illusion, or he had misidentified one or more sunspots as a planet. (Figure 15) Another possibility is that he observed one of the few asteroids with orbits that take them between the Sun and the Earth. Urbain Leverrier remained virtually the only astronomer who continued to believe in Vulcan's existence—a belief he maintained until his death in 1877.

The oddities in Mercury's orbit remained one of the major astronomical mysteries for many years. Then, in 1915, the great physicist

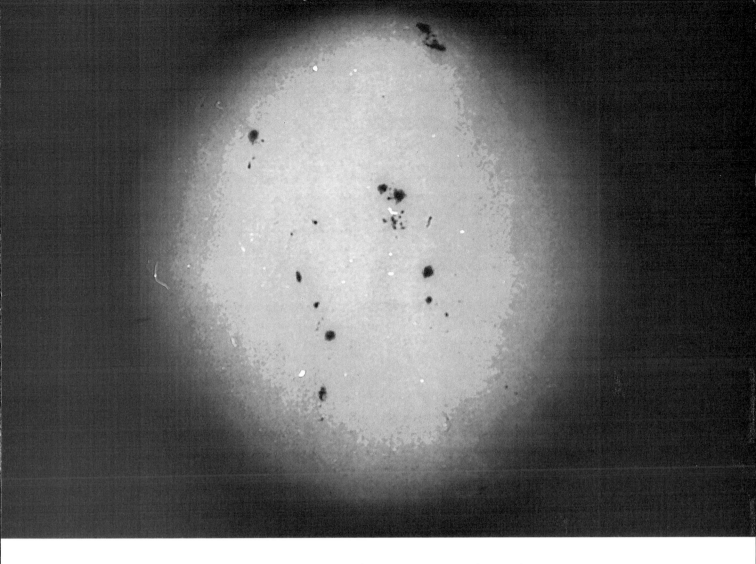

During certain periods the Sun has more sunspots than usual,
as this picture from 1937 demonstrates.

Albert Einstein announced his General Theory of Relativity, which was published the next year. Einstein explained that space is a kind of plastic substance that can change shape. The Sun's gravitation slightly curves the space near it, and this change in the geometry of space slightly alters Mercury's orbit.

Professor Einstein was not easily excited, but when he realized that he had answered one of astronomy's most puzzling questions, he wrote to a friend: "Imagine my joy . . . that my equations account for the motion of Mercury. For a few days, I was beside myself with joyous excitement."

SEVEN

PERCIVAL LOWELL AND "PLANET X"

I have now completed my investigation, and I find evidence of an exterior planet [a planet beyond Neptune] at 47.5 astronomical units [4.4 billion miles] from the Sun.

Percival Lowell, writing in 1909

✸ Astronomers made one important discovery after another in the mid- and late 1800s. By 1850, they had begun measuring the distances between Earth and the stars beyond the Sun. The numbers were enormous. Proxima Centauri, the *nearest* star to the Sun, was found to be 25,000,000,000,000 (25 trillion) miles away—9,000 times farther from the sun than Neptune. If we could shrink the Universe until the Sun was the size of the period at the end of this sentence, the star nearest to the Sun would be a period at the end of a sentence about ten miles away.

So vast are the distances between stars that astronomers felt awkward presenting them in miles. By the 1880s, they were using a new unit of measure—the *light-year*—to express gigantic distances. (Figure 16) Sound travels a fifth of a mile per second, which is why we hear the clap of thunder after we see the flash of lightning. Light also takes time to reach us, but it travels 186,000 miles per second—a million times

The canals of Mars, as drawn by Giovanni Schiaparelli (1835–1910).

faster than sound. Light from the Moon, 240,000 miles from Earth, takes a second and a quarter to reach us, while light from the Sun, 93 million miles from our planet, requires eight minutes of travel time. A light-year is the distance that light, moving at 186,000 miles per second, travels in a year, and is equal to 5,880,000,000,000 (5.88 trillion) miles. Instead of saying that Proxima Centauri is 25 trillion miles away, astronomers say that the star nearest the Sun is 4.3 light-years away, meaning that its light takes 4.3 years to reach us. Other stars were found to be hundreds or thousands of light-years distant.

Another development of the 1880s was that photography became an important astronomical tool. The great advantage of astrophotography is that a camera attached to a telescope can record details too faint to be seen through a telescope with the eye alone. Distant telescopic objects that an astronomer could barely detect often showed up bright and clear in astrophotographs.

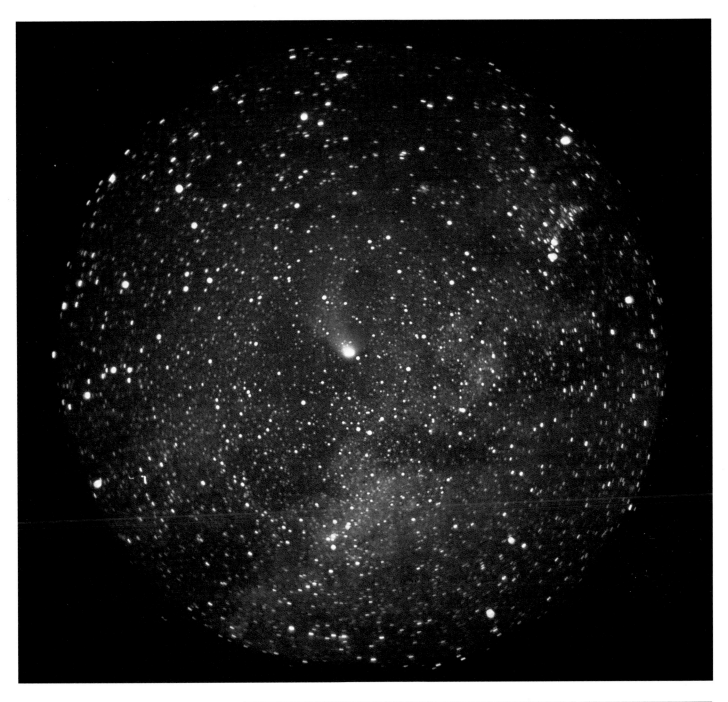

Above: **Figure 1.** Stars as seen through a telescope.

Right: **Figure 2.** The Moon and three planets. Venus is the brightest planet at right. Mars is at top and Jupiter is below Mars.

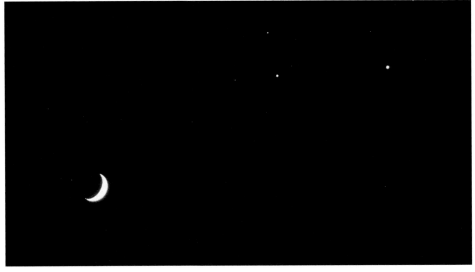

Above: **Figure 3.** The Moon.

Left: **Figure 4.** "Star trails," obtained by taking a time-exposure photograph of the night sky. The stars appear to cross the sky in an arc from east to west because the Earth is spinning.

Opposite left top: **Figure 5.** Planet Earth, as seen from the Moon.

Opposite right top: **Figure 6.** Venus.

Opposite right: **Figure 7.** Mercury.

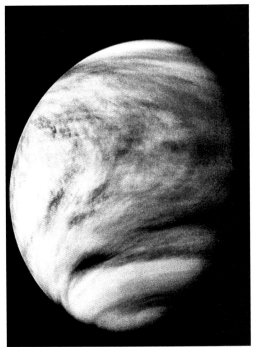

Figure 8. Earth.

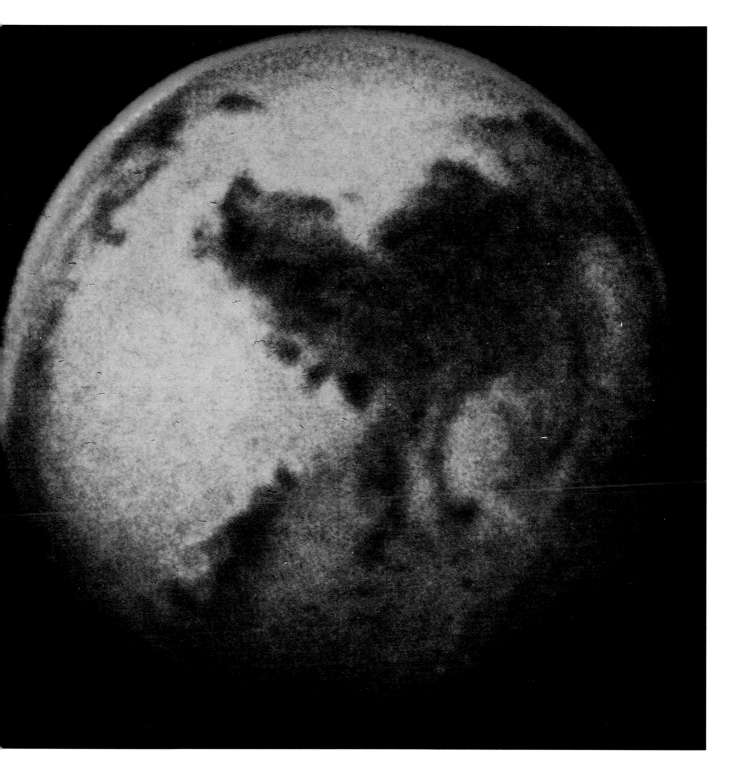

Figure 9. Mars.

Left: **Figure 10.** Jupiter.

Below: **Figure 11.** Saturn.

Opposite left top: **Figure 12.**
Close-up view of the planet Uranus.

Opposite right top: **Figure 13.** Galileo,
the first spacecraft to visit an asteroid,
took this photograph of an asteriod in
1993. The thirty-five-mile-long asteroid,
called Ida, was discovered to have a tiny
asteroid revolving around it like a moon
(seen at top). Named Dactyl, the one-
mile-wide object is the Solar System's
smallest body ever photographed up
close.

Opposite bottom: **Figure 14.**
Close-up view of the planet Neptune.

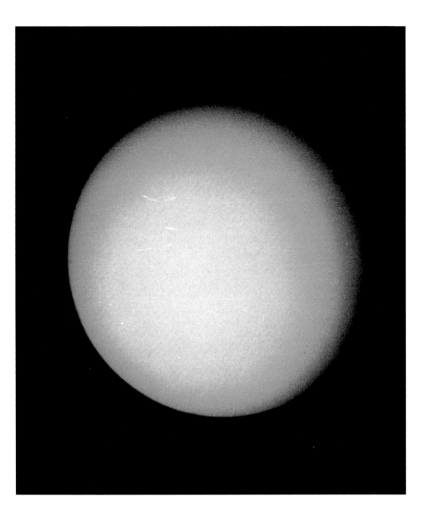

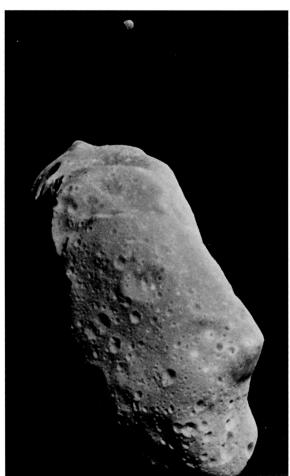

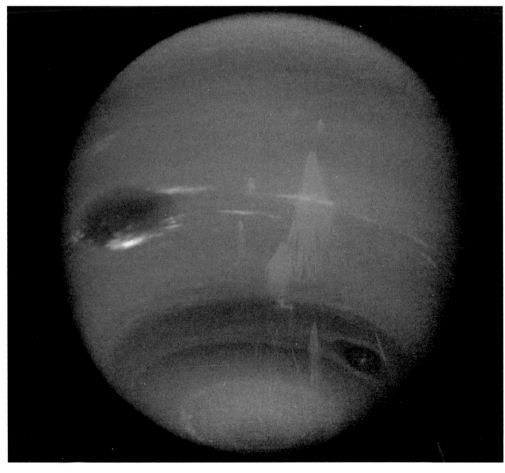

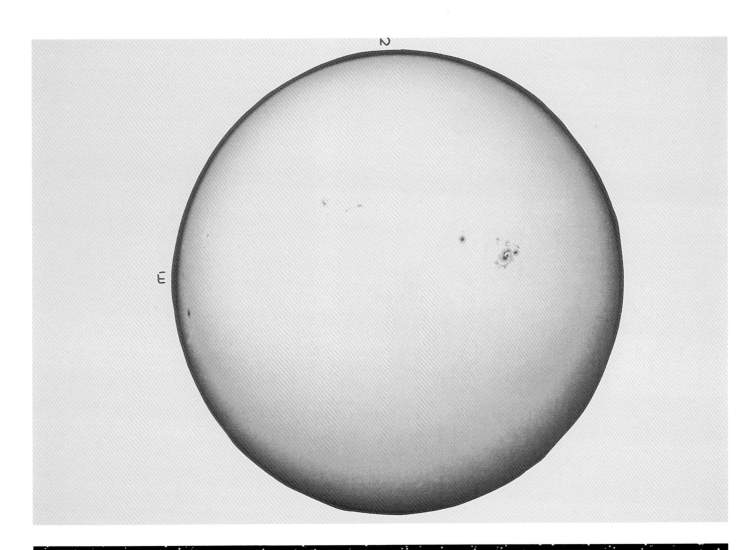

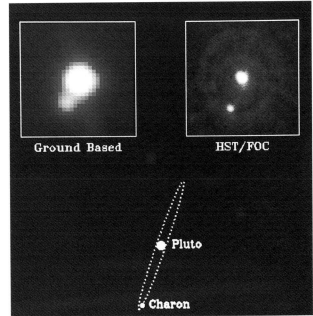

Ground Based   HST/FOC

Pluto

Charon

Opposite top: **Figure 15.** Sunspots can have unusual shapes, as the rare spiral sunspot at right shows.

Opposite bottom: **Figure 16.** Stars are so far away that we measure their distances in light-years.

Top left: **Figure 17.** Artist's conception of Pluto (the large object in the foreground) and its moon (at right) with the Sun in the distance (at top). Because Pluto is so far away from the Sun, the Sun would look much smaller and dimmer from Pluto than it does from Earth.

Top right: **Figure 18.** Two images of Pluto and its moon, Charon. The image on the left was taken by an Earth-based telescope, while the image on the right was taken by the Hubble Space Telescope.

Right: **Figure 19.** Comets develop beautiful tails when they approach the Sun.

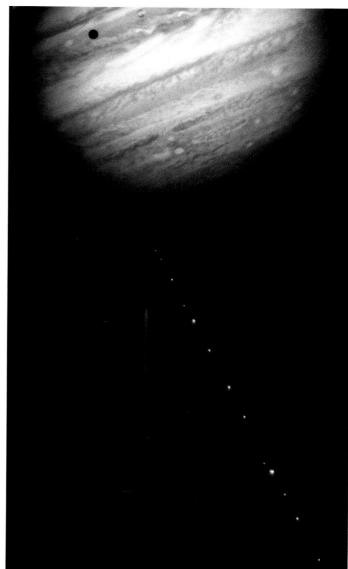

Above left: **Figure 20.** A comet.

Above right: **Figure 21.** Fragments of Comet Shoemaker-Levy headed on a collision course with Jupiter.

Left: **Figure 22.** Jupiter's "Great Comet Crash" of 1994. The dark spots are impact sites where fragments of the comet struck the giant planet.

Opposite top: **Figure 23.** Artist's conception of a comet about to crash into Washington, D.C.

Opposite bottom: **Figure 24.** A photograph of the surface of Mars, taken by one of the two Viking probes that landed on the red planet in 1976.

Opposite: **Figure 25.** Artist's depiction of two stars approaching each other.

Top: **Figure 26.** Most scientists think the Solar System formed from a single cloud of gas, dust, and ice.

Above: **Figure 27.** The spectrum of the Sun.

Figure 28. Artistic recreation of what 51
Peg and its planet might look like from
up close.

Left: **Figure 29.** Artist's preview of what a twenty-first–century space colony might look like.

Below: **Figure 30.** One day we may discover and perhaps visit an Earthlike planet such as the one shown in this artist's rendition.

Figure 31. The deepest view of the Universe ever obtained, as seen in a 1995 Hubble Space Telescope photograph. More than 1,500 galaxies, some up to 19 billion light-years away, are shown. Since the Universe is an estimated 20 billion years old, this means we are seeing galaxies as they appeared soon after the Universe began.

The late 1800s were exciting times for people interested in the planets, too. No new planets were discovered, but there was plenty of speculation about the eight that were already known. There was a popular belief—even held by some scientists—that life was possible just about anywhere. Venus, which was nicknamed "Earth's Twin" because it resembles our planet in size, was widely thought to be much like the Earth of long ago, with dinosaurs and perhaps intelligent lizardlike creatures beneath its veil of clouds. Some authors claimed that Jupiter and Saturn, which are far larger than Earth, were home to giants.

Partly due to the mistranslation of a single word, most people became convinced that Mars was home to intelligent life. In 1877 the Italian astronomer Giovanni Schiaparelli reported seeing straight lines crisscrossing Mars. He called these *canali*, an Italian word that means "channels" and can refer to natural riverbeds. However, the word was translated into the English word *canals*, which refers to man-made waterways. The news spread that a prominent astronomer had seen, with his own eyes, canals built by Martians. This began a mania for Martians that hasn't died out to this day.

Science-fiction stories about Martians became the rage. In 1898 the English author H. G. Wells published his famous novel *The War of the Worlds* about a Martian invasion of Earth. Fantastic schemes, few of which were ever attempted, were hatched to communicate with the Martians. One proposal was to build a network of mirrors across Europe in order to flash reflections of the Sun to Mars as messages. Another was to construct a twenty-mile-wide ditch in the Sahara Desert, fill it with kerosene, and set it ablaze. Other people wanted to plant gigantic forests and wheat fields in geometric shapes that the Martians could see with their telescopes.

By the 1890s Giovanni Schiaparelli's eyesight was failing, and another astronomer was needed to continue the study of the Martian canals. Percival Lowell stepped forward to pick up the

Opposite page: Illustration that accompanied H. G. Wells's writings about life on Mars.

61

torch, and in the process became a planet hunter.

Born in Boston, Massachusetts, in 1855, Percival Lowell belonged to one of the country's most prominent and gifted families. One illustrious relative, Francis Cabot Lowell, helped found America's modern cotton industry and was the man for whom Lowell, Massachusetts, was named. Percival's grandfather was the United States minister to Great Britain, while his sister, Amy Lowell, became a Pulitzer Prize–winning poet. The Lowells were related to the Cabots, which made Percival very special indeed according to a rhyme that was popular around Boston:

> *And this is good old Boston,*
> *The home of the bean and the cod,*
> *Where the Lowells talk to the Cabots,*
> *And the Cabots talk only to God.*

As a child, Percival traveled extensively with his family in Europe, which fostered two of his remarkable traits: a lifelong ability to feel at home anywhere on Earth, and a gift for learning foreign languages quickly. Once when he was about twelve years old, Percival was overheard composing verses about an imaginary shipwreck as he sailed a toy boat in a pond. What amazed his family was that his rhymes were in Latin! Soon after, Percival became interested in astronomy. His father owned a small telescope, which Percival took up to the roof of their home outside of Boston. He loved to observe Mars, which even through the small instrument revealed its white polar caps and green patches then believed to be plants. Percival was expected to enter the business world, though, so for more than twenty years astronomy remained only a hobby.

Percival Lowell accomplished a great deal during those two decades. Like many other Lowells he attended Harvard, the nation's oldest college, where he excelled at Latin, Greek, physics, and mathematics. After graduating in 1876, he worked in the family business, developing cotton mills and electric companies and managing trust funds. He yearned to travel, however, so in 1883 he sailed to the Far East, spending much of the next ten years in Japan and Korea. His knowledge of Asian customs and languages won him friends wherever he went. In Korea, which was called the "Hermit Kingdom" because it was cut off from the outside world, he was befriended by the king. Lowell was appointed as Korea's first ambassador to the United States, placing him in the strange position of representing a foreign government in his home country. Lowell wrote extensively, both while abroad and back in America. His books included *Soul of the Far East*, one of the first works by an American that demonstrated an understanding of Asian cultures.

Percival Lowell (1855–1916)

When Lowell returned to the Far East in 1891, he brought along a small telescope with which he observed Mars and Saturn. These observations seem to have strengthened his love for astronomy, for when he came home in late 1893, thirty-eight-year-old Percival Lowell shocked his friends and family with his new plans. Instead of lecturing on the

Far East or reentering the business world, he would devote his life to studying Mars. Lowell decided to build the world's foremost observatory for studying the red planet. In search of a place where the "seeing" (quality of air) was best, he investigated sites in various parts of the world. His final selection for his observatory site was a mountainous area near the young town of Flagstaff, Arizona, "far from the smoke of men." At the time, only 100,000 people lived in the Arizona Territory—just one person per square mile—so pollution and city lights were no problem. Also, Arizona's skies are clear nearly 90 percent of the time, more often than in any part of the United States.

Lowell hired workmen to build his observatory, and he assembled a staff of astronomers. On June 1, 1894—just six weeks after ground was broken—Lowell Observatory opened. Its site became known as "Mars Hill" because of Lowell's studies of the red planet with his large telescopes.

Lowell and his staff observed the more than one hundred *canali* that Giovanni Schiaparelli had seen, and they also mapped about four hundred more. As they had with William Herschel, many professional astronomers viewed Lowell as a hobbyist who didn't belong in their domain. In turn, Lowell resented the charge some astronomers made that the canals he described were telescopic illusions. "In good air they stand out at times with startling abruptness," he wrote. One waterway Lowell reported seeing was more than 3,500 miles long—quite impressive, considering that the longest irrigation canal on Earth today, the Karakumsky Canal in the former Soviet Union, extends 745 miles, or about a fifth of that length.

As Lowell mapped the canals, it became clear to him that they radiated in every direction from the planet's white polar caps. William H. Pickering, an astronomer who had helped Lowell found the observatory, made a further discovery. Round, dark spots seemed to be located on Mars at places where a number of canals met. Lowell and his staff counted about two hundred of these dark spots, one of them situated where seventeen canals converged.

Percival Lowell formulated a theory about Mars. The red planet, he claimed, was populated by beings similar to us Earthlings. However, Mars was a dying world, where water was in short supply. The Martians solved this problem by digging a network of canals through which they pumped water from their planet's polar ice. Lowell concluded that the dark spots were cities, which had been built in places where many canals came together because the inhabitants needed large supplies of water. He agreed with other astronomers that the greenish patches on Mars were plants.

The public gobbled up Lowell's theory. Wherever he lectured about the Martians, huge audiences packed the halls. One of his most appealing ideas was that the Martians had learned to live in peace, as shown by the "fact" that building a huge canal system must have required global cooperation. Percival Lowell also wrote books on the red planet—*Mars* (1895), *Mars and Its Canals* (1906), and *Mars as the Abode of Life* (1908). He helped convince so many people of the existence of intelligent life on Mars that a contest offering a prize to the first person to contact extraterrestrials (beings from beyond Earth) excluded Martians. Finding them was thought to be too easy!

Thanks to his work on Mars, Percival Lowell became the world's biggest astronomical "star." But he was deeply hurt that many scientists continued to claim that his imagination was getting the best of him when he interpreted lines and dots as canals and cities. Lowell decided that he needed to boost his reputation and, as Lowell Observatory astronomer Dr. Carl Lampland phrased it, "gain more respectability for his theories about Mars." Percival Lowell then turned to a topic involving such hard work and difficult calculation that it was certain to win the respect of other scientists: the search for a ninth planet.

Astronomers had begun to think about a ninth planet soon after the discovery of Neptune in 1846. The reason was that neither Uranus nor Neptune behaved as it should. Some object besides Neptune seemed to be tugging at Uranus, and Neptune itself seemed to be pulled from the outside by an unknown planet. In the late 1800s several astronomers searched the sky for a "trans-Neptunian planet" (meaning a planet beyond Neptune), but the new century began and the missing planet remained undiscovered.

Percival Lowell started his planet hunt in 1905. His observatory staff photographed parts of the sky where he suspected the planet might be. Using a magnifying glass, Lowell examined pairs of photographic plates taken of the same portion of sky over time. Objects that appeared in the same positions relative to each other on both plates he knew to be stars. What he was looking for was an object that shifted position slightly from plate to plate, for it might be a distant planet orbiting the Sun. Lowell began referring to the subject of his search as "Planet X," because in science, "X" means the unknown. As he made new calculations, Lowell had his assistants photograph new areas of the sky. By 1908, he had studied 440 photographic plates without discovering Planet X.

In late 1908, Lowell attended a lecture by William H. Pickering, who had helped found Lowell Observatory. Pickering, who had left the observatory in 1895, had begun to doubt Lowell's theory about life on Mars. Not only that, he had decided to compete with his former employer at planet hunting. At his lecture, Pickering spoke about his predictions for a ninth planet, which he called Planet O, but he didn't stop there. Over the next few years he predicted the locations of several other trans-Neptunian planets, including Planets P, Q, R, S, T, and U! Pickering seemed determined to make so many predictions that one was bound to come true. Yet Pickering's rivalry with him helped Lowell, for it inspired him to

Opposite page: Percival Lowell spent many hours in his observatory studying Mars.

refine his calculations and intensify his search for Planet X.

Lowell resumed his hunt for Planet X in 1910. This time to aid him in the project he bought a Blink-Microscope-Comparator, a device that magnifies astrophotographs and allows the observer to rapidly compare two pictures of the same area of the sky. As the observer looks through the Comparator eyepiece, the device provides alternate views of first one photograph and then another. If only stars are on the two photographic plates, both pictures will look identical. But if a planet has been photographed, it will appear to move back and forth, wandering among the background stars, as the two pictures blink on and off.

Percival Lowell continued his search for Planet X with an intensity that his friend George Russell Agassiz later claimed "virtually killed him" and with a lack of success that his brother Abbott Lawrence Lowell later called "the sharpest disappointment of his life." From April of 1914 to July of 1916, nearly a thousand photographic plates—about five hundred pairs—were taken of areas of the sky where Lowell thought the ninth planet might be located. During this period an undiscovered planet did actually appear on two of his photographic plates, but the distant world was in an extremely starry portion of the Milky Way. When the plates were "blinked" in the Comparator, Lowell's staff missed seeing the planet jump back and forth.

Lowell spent his last years working at a furious pace. Besides hunting for the ninth planet, he lectured extensively on Mars, wrote books and articles, and served as professor of astronomy at Massachusetts Institute of Technology (MIT). On November 12, 1916, Percival Lowell suffered a stroke and died at his observatory. He was buried on Mars Hill, near the telescope he had used in the work that made him famous: his studies of the red planet, Mars.

EIGHT

"I HAVE FOUND YOUR PLANET X!"

When I came across the images, I said "That's it!" to myself. It was a super super moment, a moment of great elation and excitement.

Clyde Tombaugh, recalling the moment that he discovered Pluto in 1930

✸ Percival Lowell bequeathed more than a million dollars—most of his fortune—to his observatory. However, he had married a few years before his death, and Constance Lowell was wounded that he had left more money for the upkeep of his observatory than to her. She fought the will, so that by the time Lowell's estate was finally settled in 1927, lawyers' fees and court costs had swallowed up much of the money. The long court battle was a major reason why Lowell Observatory suspended its Planet X search for thirteen years following Lowell's death.

Meanwhile, William H. Pickering was still trying to discover the trans-Neptunian planet, but, like Adams and Leverrier nearly a century earlier, he couldn't convince an observatory to conduct a major search based on his calculations. In the March 1929 issue of *Popular Astronomy* magazine, seventy-one-year-old Pickering pleaded for an observatory to hunt for his planet, but by then he had used up so many letters of the alphabet with his numerous planetary predictions that

The Whirlpool Galaxy.

his reputation had suffered. That same issue of *Popular Astronomy* also contained an article by Vesto Slipher, who had taken over as the director of Lowell Observatory. With Lowell's estate finally settled, the observatory was about to begin a new Planet X search. Lowell's family felt that finding the planet would be a fitting memorial to "Uncle Percy," so his brother Dr. Abbott Lawrence Lowell, president of Harvard University, donated $10,000 to build a thirteen-inch refractor especially designed to photograph the sky in a planetary hunt.

In many ways, the time no longer seemed ripe for a Planet X

search, for by the 1920s most astronomers were interested in more distant objects. Ever since William Herschel described seeing "telescopic Milky Ways," many astronomers believed that countless galaxies (groups of billions of stars moving together through space) similar to the Milky Way must be scattered about the Universe. This was finally proved in 1924, when American astronomer Edwin Hubble showed that a blob of light in the constellation Andromeda was another galaxy. The Andromeda Galaxy was found to be twice the size of our Milky Way Galaxy and was located a mind-boggling *two million* light-years from the Sun. Other galaxies were discovered to be much farther still. The Lowell Observatory staff entered the new field of galactic studies and also wanted to continue their founder's research on Mars. Vesto Slipher decided that an assistant astronomer should be hired to photograph the sky for the Planet X project.

Slipher knew what kind of person he wanted. Photographing the night sky could require years of difficult and slow work, so the astronomer had to be energetic and able to stick to a project. The photography had to be high quality, and each pair of plates had to be taken days apart yet show the same exact region of the sky, so the assistant had to be careful and methodical. Furthermore, because a veteran astronomer might move on to pursue other interests, the best person for the job would be an eager and ambitious young person happy to be working at a major observatory. Money was a factor, too, for the observatory couldn't afford to hire another established astronomer. Slipher felt that the young assistant would be a kind of hired workman carrying out Lowell's plan, and that the observatory's founder would receive nearly all of the credit if the planet were located.

As Vesto Slipher searched for the right person for the job, he received a letter from a twenty-two-year-old amateur astronomer who lived on a Kansas farm. His name was Clyde Tombaugh, and he had enclosed a number of drawings of Mars and Jupiter as those planets appeared through his telescope. Clyde soon received a letter from Slipher asking information about himself, including the odd question: "Are you in good health?" Clyde didn't know it yet, but Slipher was hoping he had found his planet hunter.

The discoverers of Uranus and Neptune lived long ago, so we must consult books to learn about them. But to learn about Clyde Tombaugh, in late 1995 I visited him at his home, across the road from a horse farm near Las Cruces, New Mexico. Although he was approaching his ninetieth birthday and needed to carry around an oxygen tank for a heart condition, Clyde was a lively, friendly man who cracked jokes at every opportunity. He greeted me by saying: "I like living close to horses because they make such good *neigh*-bors!"

Clyde William Tombaugh was born on a farm near Streator, Illinois, eighty miles southwest of Chicago, on February 4, 1906. He was the oldest of six children in a family that grew corn and wheat. "On the farm in those days we didn't have labor-saving machinery, so you either worked hard or you didn't survive," Clyde recalled. The kind of boy who kept track of everything he did, he once figured that he had husked 7,000 bushels (400,000 pounds) of corn over several years. "Farming trained me to work hard and long," he explained.

In the two-room schoolhouse Clyde attended, history and geography were his favorite subjects. One day in sixth grade, he realized that he knew a great deal about the Earth's geography but little about the other planets. He began taking astronomy books out of the Streator Library. "I loved to read about William Herschel, who became one of my heroes," continued Clyde. "I admired his persistence, which helped him discover Uranus and understand the Milky Way. Also, I enjoyed reading about Adams and Leverrier and the Neptune controversy, and about Percival Lowell and the canals of Mars."

Clyde first gazed through a telescope when he was twelve years old. The instrument, his uncle's, had a magnifying power of only 36, yet it

Clyde Tombaugh (1906-1997) in 1910. The future astronomer is wearing the hat. He is pictured with his parents and his little sister, Esther.

provided breathtaking views of the Moon. Two years later, in 1920, Clyde's uncle and father bought a better telescope from Sears Roebuck that they shared. Studying Mars through this instrument, Clyde was mesmerized by the planet's greenish patches and white polar cap—just as Percival Lowell had been while observing from his rooftop fifty years earlier.

When Clyde was sixteen, he and his family moved to a farm near Burdett, Kansas, where they grew wheat and a cornlike plant called kafir. The teenager devoted his evenings to astronomy. His father and uncle gave Clyde their telescope, which he used to observe the heavens on clear nights. On cloudy nights, Clyde read astronomy books by the light of a kerosene lamp. But he wasn't only a bookworm. He played baseball and football and set up his own pole-vaulting course at home. One day as he was in the midst of a vault, his home-

made pole broke. Fortunately for Clyde—and for the discovery of the ninth planet—he avoided being speared by the pole as he landed.

Following high school graduation in 1925, Clyde continued to work on the family farm. Although his family couldn't afford to send him to college, he decided that he needed larger telescopes in order to be more like a real astronomer. "I couldn't afford to buy telescopes, so I began to make them," he explained. In 1928 he completed a nine-inch reflector—quite an achievement for a twenty-two-year-old amateur astronomer. Clyde studied the planets and stars in far greater detail with this telescope than he had as a boy.

Life was extremely difficult for American farmers in the late 1920s and early 1930s. Bad weather and the low prices paid for agricultural products cost many families their farms. In June of 1928 a hailstorm destroyed the Tombaughs' crops. "Farming is not for me," Clyde sadly told his parents. "The first chance I have of getting out of it, I'm going."

Clyde thought of two possible jobs. He could set up a small telescope-making business, or he could work for the railroad in the hope of becoming a train engineer. While pondering his future, he sent several drawings of Mars and Jupiter to Lowell Observatory in late 1928, in the hope of receiving a little encouragement. After an exchange of several letters, Clyde received great news in the mail. Dr. Slipher wanted to know: "Would you be interested in coming to Flagstaff on a few months' trial basis, about the middle of January?" Recognizing that this was the opportunity of a lifetime, the young Kansan accepted, despite not yet knowing what kind of work he would be doing.

On a January day in 1929, Clyde said good-bye to his family and boarded the train bound for a strange place a thousand miles away where he didn't know a soul. It took Clyde twenty-eight hours to reach Flagstaff, Arizona. His fears were eased a little when a gray-haired man at the station introduced himself as Vesto Slipher and asked, "Are you

Opposite page: Twenty-two-year-old Tombaugh with the nine-inch reflector he completed in 1928.

Clyde Tombaugh?" As Slipher drove him up Mars Hill to the famous observatory, Clyde still had no clue as to why he had been hired.

The next day Slipher finally explained that Clyde was to work on an important project: the search for Percival Lowell's Planet X. Each night when moonlight or clouds didn't interfere, Clyde was to photograph part of the sky, making sure to cover the region where Lowell claimed the planet would be, plus other places along the Zodiac, and to photograph each area several days apart. Vesto Slipher and the other experienced astronomers planned to take turns studying each pair of photographic plates in the Blink-Microscope-Comparator. That part of the search carried the most responsibility, for a lapse in concentration of even one second could result in the planet being missed in the viewer. As the rookie astronomer on the staff, Clyde was also to conduct observatory tours for visitors each weekday afternoon.

Clyde had to wait a few weeks for the special planetary search telescope to be completed and installed. As he did so, he began to realize that Dr. Vesto Slipher and the rest of the staff were not optimistic about the project. "They were discouraged," Tombaugh remembered. "That made me doubtful about success, yet I felt I should just go about my job because it was better than making hay at home!" When Clyde studied Percival Lowell's earlier searches, he became more hopeful—not because they were so carefully done but because they were rather haphazard. "I hate to say it, but the searches for Planet X at Lowell Observatory had been sloppily done. I'm a perfectionist. I decided to do the project as carefully as possible, and if I found nothing through the whole Zodiac, then the ninth planet simply didn't exist."

On April 6, 1929, Tombaugh began photographing the sky. After a lapse of thirteen years, Lowell Observatory's hunt for Planet X was once again in full swing. As the weeks passed, Dr. Slipher was pleased with Clyde Tombaugh's picturetaking, but Tombaugh was disappointed in the other aspect of the search. The veteran astronomers lacked the time and patience for studying the photographic plates in the Comparator, so that few of the plates had been blinked by mid-June. Around then, Dr. Slipher surprised Tombaugh by assigning him the most important task in the planet search. Besides taking the nightly photographs, he was to blink them in the Comparator. "When I began to do the blinking, I felt that I had taken over the entire project," Tombaugh explained.

Blinking the photographs was so difficult that Tombaugh compared it to looking for a needle in a cosmic haystack. The average photographic plate contained 160,000 stars, and some plates taken of regions around the middle of the Milky Way contained a *million* stars. "To this day, people don't realize what was involved," Tombaugh told me, and demonstrated his point by placing an old photographic plate with close to a million stars on it upon his dining room table.

He couldn't study all the stars on a plate at once, so Tombaugh divided each picture into sections of several hundred stars for analysis on the Comparator. Another obstacle to picking out a planet among the huge number of stars was that there were many false leads. The photographic process often produces small specks on photos that can resemble stars. Asteroids were even more bothersome, for they orbit the Sun, and, similarly to planets, change position from picture to picture. Johannes Kepler's Third Law—bodies move slower when farther from the Sun—helped Tombaugh distinguish asteroids from Planet X. Located between Mars and Jupiter, asteroids could be identified because they moved at a faster rate than a trans-Neptunian planet.

The Young Kansan had been working on the project for about three months when an elderly astronomer from the East visited Lowell Observatory. He was talking to Dr. Slipher and Tombaugh about the Planet X search when Slipher was called to the telephone. Once alone with him, the astronomer leaned over to Tombaugh and quietly advised: "Young man, I am afraid you are wasting your time. If

Clyde Tombaugh at work "blinking" photographic plates as he searches for the ninth planet.

there were any more planets to be found, they would have been found long before this." Tombaugh feared that the man might be right, but he answered: "We have one of the most powerful planet-search instruments in the world. I am going to give it all that I have."

Another visitor who was prowling around the observatory wasn't so easily answered. Tombaugh was working late one night when he heard a ferocious growl coming from just outside the dome. "I was pretty scared when I realized that it was a mountain lion!" he recalled. His worst fear was that it would climb inside the dome through the overhead slit that revealed a portion of the sky. Despite his terror, he finished taking his photograph before dashing to the safety of the observatory's administration building.

Later in the summer the cloudy season began and Tombaugh was allowed a three-week vacation. He went home and helped with the wheat harvest. Never had he enjoyed farmwork more. After spending his nights alone with a telescope and many long hours sifting through millions of star images, he was happy to be back with his family and working close to the earth.

He returned to the observatory refreshed and eager to continue his search. Week after week he photographed the sky, moving eastward through the constellations Aquarius, Pisces, Aries, and Taurus. Generally he awoke at noon, ate breakfast, showed visitors around the observatory, and spent much of the afternoon developing the photographic plates he had taken the previous night. On some afternoons and also on evenings when observing conditions were poor, he did the blinking with the Comparator. Late into the night when conditions permitted he took new photographs of the sky.

By early 1930, when he had been at the observatory for about a year, Tombaugh was photographing the sky in the region of the constellation Gemini the Twins. On the nights of January 23 and 29, he photographed the area around Delta Gemini, a star called Delta Gem for short. On February 18, two weeks past his twenty-fourth birthday, he placed the Delta Gem plates in the Comparator and began blinking them. He had been studying the plates for a few hours when he noticed a dim object that had moved a short way among the stars in the six days between photographs.

"That's it!" he told himself.

The more he scrutinized the object, the more certain Tombaugh became that it was Planet X. He performed a quick calculation based on its small amount of movement and figured that it was located per-

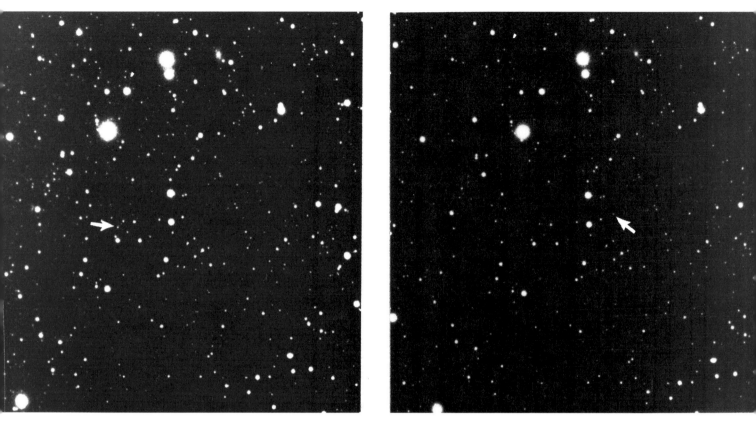

The plates on which Tombaugh discovered Pluto. The planet is the dim object that moved slightly among the stars from one plate to the next.

haps a billion miles beyond Neptune. He also checked his watch and noted the time of discovery: 4:00 P.M., Tuesday, February 18, 1930.

Clyde Tombaugh looked back on his discovery of the ninth planet more than sixty-five years ago as "a super super moment, a moment of great elation." He rushed down the hall to Vesto Slipher's office and announced, "Dr. Slipher, I have found your Planet X!" Slipher instantly rose from his chair with a look on his face of both excitement and doubt. "I'll show you the evidence," Tombaugh reassured him.

Tombaugh could barely keep up with Slipher as the observatory director hurried to the Comparator room. As Slipher viewed the January 23 and 29 Delta Gem plates in the machine and watched the little object jump back and forth, Tombaugh explained, "The shift, in my opinion, indicates that the object is well beyond the orbit of Neptune."

Slipher agreed that the object was almost certainly the ninth planet, but he wanted absolute proof before releasing the news to the world. "This could be very hot news," Slipher told Tombaugh. "Don't tell anyone until we follow it for a few weeks, and rephotograph the region as soon as possible."

Clyde would have given just about anything to rephotograph the planet suspect that night, but the day had been cloudy. Glancing out of the window, he saw that there was no change in the weather. "Doesn't look very good for tonight," Clyde said to Slipher, yet he still clung to a slim hope that the clouds would break.

Late that afternoon, Tombaugh drove the observatory's old Model T Ford down to Flagstaff to pick up the observatory's mail and eat at the Black Cat Cafe. Usually Clyde was a calm person, but as he ate dinner that evening his knees trembled. All he needed was for the clouds to clear to verify the biggest astronomical discovery since the discovery of Neptune eighty-four years earlier.

After dinner, he went outside and looked up at the sky. Not a single star was visible through the thick clouds. He yearned to phone a relative or friend to share his news, but he obeyed Slipher's order to keep it a secret. He knew that if the news leaked, another astronomer might hear about it and try to snatch the credit for the discovery from Lowell Observatory.

Tombaugh decided to see a movie while waiting for a break in the clouds. He drove to the Orpheum Theater, where, for the next hour and a half, he watched *The Virginian*, a 1929 Western starring Gary Cooper. He couldn't concentrate on the plot, though, for he was thinking about the distant world behind the clouds. After the film ended, Clyde left the theater and glanced upward once again. The sky was still cloudy.

He returned to the observatory and spent several hours studying books by Percival Lowell, interrupting his reading repeatedly to check the sky. By two o'clock, he knew it was useless. Even if the clouds passed, the planet would be too far west to photograph, and, besides, the rising Moon would have blotted out the dim object. Clyde then went to bed, too excited to get much sleep.

The next morning, February 19, the sky seemed to be brightening. Tombaugh spent a tense day watching the sky clear and counting the hours until nightfall. That evening there was a mist in the air, but the stars were bright and clear. He aimed the telescope and camera at the Delta Gem region, and by midnight he had completed a photographic plate, which he immediately developed and dried. As he placed the photograph in the Comparator along with one of the earlier plates from January, he knew that the next few moments would reveal whether or not he had discovered a new planet.

Almost instantly he saw it. As the two photographic plates blinked on and off, a small object shifted back and forth about four-tenths of an inch (one centimeter). The object was in exactly the position it should be if it lay beyond Neptune's orbit. When Dr. Slipher saw the new photographic plate, he knew that the ninth planet had been discovered. However, Slipher wanted everyone to remember that Percival Lowell had predicted the planet's existence, so he waited several weeks until a historic date to announce the discovery. On March 13, 1930—the day that would have been Percival Lowell's seventy-fifth birthday as well as the 149th anniversary of William Herschel's discovery of Uranus—the observatory issued a statement about the new planet:

> *The finding of this object was a direct result of the search program set going in 1905 by Dr. Lowell in connection with his work on the evidence of a planet beyond Neptune. . . . Its position and distance appear to fit only those of an object*

beyond Neptune, and . . . apparently fulfill Lowell's theoretical findings.

"I realized I had been hunting big game and that the discovery would be flooding the news," Clyde Tombaugh explained, but even he was surprised by the worldwide headlines over the next few days. The story was especially big in the United States, for the planet was the first ever discovered from that nation. Under its front-page headline, SEE ANOTHER WORLD IN SKY, the March 14 *Chicago Tribune* asserted that "astronomically, the discovery is regarded as the greatest since the location of Neptune, eighth member of the Solar System, in 1846." The March 14 *New York Times*, which ran a page-one article headlined NINTH PLANET DISCOVERED ON EDGE OF SOLAR SYSTEM, was even more lavish in its praise. The *Times* reminded its readers that the ninth planet had been far more difficult to locate than the eighth, and called the discovery "one of the greatest events in the history of [astronomy]." In its article THE NEW PLANET, the March 15 *London Times* informed its readers that "all the observations indicate that the object is the one which Dr. Lowell saw mathematically."

Because the newspapers obtained most of their information from Lowell Observatory, all of the articles had three things in common. The reporters awarded the bulk of the credit to Percival Lowell, going so far as to say that he mathematically "saw" the planet, when the proper word was "predicted." They either neglected to mention Clyde Tombaugh, or merely identified him as the "observatory photographer." And third, the articles contained a great deal of misinformation about the new planet. One mistake that would prove critical was its size. Percival Lowell had estimated Planet X to be very large, so newspapers speculated that it was "perhaps bigger than Jupiter," which has a diameter of 89,000 miles. Were that true, the object would have been the largest of the nine planets. Actually, it was the smallest, and could fit inside Jupiter more than 100,000 times!

Although barely mentioned at first, Clyde Tombaugh was proud of his role in the discovery, and of the fact that he had helped bestow glory on Percival Lowell's memory. Writers and astronomers came to Mars Hill to interview him, and gradually the world learned that a twenty-four-year-old assistant who hadn't even gone to college had located the new planet. Thousands of vacationers also came to Lowell Observatory to see the place where the discovery had been made. Since Tombaugh was still conducting the tours, visitors had the unique opportunity of being shown around the observatory by the man who had found the ninth planet.

More than a thousand letters suggesting names for the planet were sent to Lowell Observatory. Constance Lowell, Percival's widow, favored "Zeus," but that god was the Greek version of the Roman god Jupiter, who already had a planet named for him. Mrs. Lowell was mercurial regarding her choice of names and in rapid succession she then proposed that the planet be called "Lowell," "Percival," "Planet X," and even "Constance," for herself. Other people put forward such names as "Minerva," for the Roman goddess of wisdom, and "Hercules," for the ancient Greek hero who was said to be the strongest man on Earth.

A young girl across the Atlantic Ocean in Oxford, England, also thought up a name for the planet. At breakfast one day in March of 1930, eleven-year-old Venetia Burney and her family came across a newspaper article about the discovery of the ninth planet.

"What will be its name?" asked Venetia's grandfather.

"It might be called Pluto," answered Venetia, referring to the Greek and Roman god of the dead.

Today, at nearly eighty years of age, Venetia Burney Phair recalls in a letter to the author that she didn't expect her suggestion to go beyond her family's breakfast table. "I read a lot as a child," she explains, "and at school I was fascinated by astronomy and mythology. But after I told my family that 'Pluto' would be a good name for the planet, I didn't think any more about it for several months."

Unknown to Venetia, her grandfather and an Oxford University professor telegraphed her suggestion to Lowell Observatory. Soon after, the entire Lowell Observatory staff voted and chose Venetia Burney's suggestion, and on May 1, 1930, the name *Pluto* was officially adopted. It was a fine decision, for in mythology the god Pluto ruled over a dark, cold realm—a world much like the planet itself. Also, Pluto began with Percival Lowell's initials: PL. "After it was all settled, I was told I had named the planet," continues Venetia Burney Phair, "and of course I was very excited and pleased. Over the years, it has given me a great deal of pleasure to know that I named Pluto."

William Pickering liked the name too. He also claimed credit for helping to inspire the search, and said half jokingly that the first two letters in Pluto stood for Pickering-Lowell. The adoption of the name suggested by young Venetia Burney had other interesting consequences. On September 5, 1930, a fictional dog was introduced to the world in a Mickey Mouse cartoon. He was named Pluto, perhaps in honor of the planet.

Venetia Burney, at about the time that she named Pluto.

Shortly after the discovery of Uranus, a new element had been identified and named *uranium* for the seventh planet. Two elements that
were discovered in 1940 were named *neptunium* and *plutonium,* for
the eighth and ninth planets.

Following the discovery of Pluto, Lowell Observatory felt that
there might be more planets out there, so Clyde Tombaugh was
retained to continue the search, which he did (with time off for college) for the next thirteen years. By the time Tombaugh's planetary
hunt ended in 1943, he had produced 338 pairs of photographic
plates covering the entire Zodiac and much more of the sky border-
ing that region, and he had spent seven thousand hours at the
Comparator viewing about *90 million* star images. To this day, few
astronomers in history have studied so much of the sky in such detail
as Clyde Tombaugh.

Meanwhile, astronomers were learning some startling facts about
Pluto. It turned out that Percival Lowell's 1914 Planet X and William
Pickering's 1919 Planet O predictions were about equally accurate—
or, rather, equally inaccurate. The planet had been found fairly far (6
degrees) from where either Pickering or Lowell had claimed it would
be located. More importantly, Pluto was a fraction of the size that
either Lowell or Pickering had calculated. In fact, it was so tiny that it
couldn't possibly be causing the variations in Uranus's and Neptune's
orbits that had led astronomers to look for the ninth planet in the first
place! This meant that the discovery of Pluto was due to Clyde
Tombaugh's search rather than Percival Lowell's calculations. By the
late 1930s, astronomers had begun to adopt the attitude that prevails
today: Clyde Tombaugh discovered Pluto through his careful photography and examination of photographic plates, but some credit must
be given to Percival Lowell for initiating the search.

As Tombaugh's reputation eclipsed Percival Lowell's, Vesto Slipher
became jealous. One day Tombaugh overheard a conversation in which

Slipher downplayed Clyde's role in the discovery of Pluto to astronomer Carl Lampland. "Well," answered Lampland, taking Clyde's side, "he is the one who did the work! He did the blinking! And he is the one who found it!" The talk around the observatory was that Dr. Slipher thought that if Percival Lowell wasn't going to receive credit for discovering Pluto, he himself deserved the laurels because Tombaugh had been working under him. In 1944 Clyde was devastated when Dr. Slipher suddenly told him to "find other employment." Despite all the painstaking work he had done on the institution's behalf over fourteen years, Clyde had been fired by Lowell Observatory.

Clyde enjoyed a successful career in astronomy following his departure from the observatory. He had earned his master's degree in astronomy in 1939, and in 1955, at the age of forty-nine, he became a professor at New Mexico State University, where he helped to found the Astronomy Department. After retiring in 1973, he continued to lecture on astronomy, and in 1980, at the age of seventy-four, he published *Out of the Darkness*, a book about his discovery of Pluto. By the time I met Clyde Tombaugh, he had another distinction besides having discovered a planet. He had been married to the same woman, Patricia Edson Tombaugh, since 1934. Patricia probably deserved most of the credit for their long marriage, though, for she had to endure Clyde's corny jokes for more than sixty years. For example, over dessert at a restaurant near his and Patsy's home, Clyde told me: "Pluto is a good name for the planet because it was so doggone hard to find!"

Sadly, however, Clyde Tombaugh died in 1997 within three weeks of what would have been his ninety-first birthday. One of his last contributions in the field of astronomy was to provide pictures and information for this chapter and to check it over for accuracy.

Percival Lowell hasn't fared as well as Clyde Tombaugh in the judgment of history. Up until the 1960s, there were still many people

Clyde and Patsy Tombaugh at the time the author visited them in 1995.

who believed Lowell's ideas about canals and Martians. Then probes landed on Mars, revealing the disappointing truth. The canals and cities do not exist and were in fact telescopic illusions. Mars's greenish areas are not plants at all, but seem to be dark volcanic and rocky regions that take on a greenish color though a telescope. Furthermore, Mars has little of the oxygen needed by the higher life forms on Earth, and the red planet's temperatures plunge to -220 degrees Fahrenheit—much too cold for human-type life to survive. Today Lowell's ideas about Mars are often used as examples of how scientists can jump to conclusions. Percival Lowell's reputation now rests mainly on what began as a sidelight of his astronomical career— starting the search that led to the discovery of Pluto.

NINE

BEYOND PLUTO: IS THERE A TENTH PLANET?

There is no such body as a tenth planet [in the Solar System].

Clyde Tombaugh

My conclusion is that something not yet discovered is affecting the outer Solar System. I think it's a tenth planet.

Planet hunter Dr. Tom Van Flandern

✸ Within hours of the announcement of the discovery of Pluto in 1930, Yale University astronomer Frank Schlesinger was asked whether more planets would be found. "Other major planets will [probably] be added to our Solar System," Dr. Schlesinger predicted, "but it will be increasingly difficult to discover them, as the outer ones must be very faint as seen from Earth."

As astronomers learned more about Pluto's size, the likelihood of there being a tenth planet seemed to grow. The 1930 discovery reports estimated that the ninth planet was "certainly no smaller than the Earth," which has a diameter of eight thousand miles. (Figure 17) By the 1950s, the figure for Pluto's diameter had been revised downward to four thousand miles, roughly that of Mars. Then in 1978, Pluto's moon, Charon, was discovered. By analyzing the gravitational attraction between Pluto and its moon, astronomers determined just how small the ninth planet is. With a diameter of just 1,400 miles, Pluto is not only the smallest of the nine known planets, it is even smaller than Jupiter's four largest moons that Galileo discovered. Clearly Pluto wasn't large enough to account for the "residuals" (unexplained peculiarities) in the orbits of Uranus and Neptune. (Figure 18)

If Pluto wasn't pulling Uranus and Neptune out of position, what was? A number of astronomers concluded that a larger planet that had been predicted by Lowell or Pickering remained undiscovered and could still be found. Several planet hunters went to work to search for a tenth planet.

One major search was conducted between 1977 and 1985 at California's Palomar Observatory by Charles Kowal, who used a camera attached to a forty-eight-inch reflector to take photographic plates. "I blinked them like Clyde," Kowal explains. "During my search I discovered fifteen unusual asteroids, six comets which were named for me, and Chiron." This last body, not to be confused with Pluto's moon, Charon, helped to make Kowal famous. For a while it was thought to be the most distant known astcroid, but now it is believed to be a comet. Although Kowal did not find a tenth planet and has suspended his planet hunt for the present, he believes that another searcher may hit pay dirt: "I blinked plates for many years, examining tens of millions of stars, and I know how easy it is to miss something if you daydream for an instant. Constant alertness is not really humanly possible, so just because I didn't find it, I wouldn't rule out the possibility of a tenth planet."

Another planet hunter, Robert Harrington of the U.S. Naval Observatory, calculated that a large tenth planet was eluding astronomers because it was located in the southern sky, beyond the region where Tombaugh and Kowal had searched and south of where the other known planets are located. Harrington went to New Zealand, an island country southeast of Australia, where for several years in the late 1980s and early 1990s he photographed the southern sky. In case the tenth planet showed up as he blinked his plates in a Comparator, Harrington had a name picked out for it— Humphrey. Harrington died in 1993 without having found Humphrey, but, as will be seen, a colleague of his thinks the planet may have been in a star-rich area of the southern Milky Way where it was extremely difficult to spot.

In recent years, however, most astronomers have come to believe that there is no massive planet beyond Pluto. The *Voyager 2* space probe that approached Uranus in 1986 and Neptune in 1989 helped create this shift in opinion. Data gathered by the probe convinced many scientists that there are no residuals, or oddities, in the orbits of Uranus and Neptune, so there is no evidence that a large body beyond Pluto is pulling the two planets out of position.

Why did Lowell, Pickering, and other planet hunters believe that those residuals existed? Because they based their work on old observations and calculations that weren't accurate, explains Harvard University astronomy professor Jane Luu. Uranus takes eighty-four years, and Neptune 165 years, to orbit the Sun. Uranus has orbited the Sun only two and a half times since William Herschel discovered it in 1781, while Neptune hasn't even completed one orbit since its discovery in 1846. Astrophotography had not yet been invented when Uranus and Neptune were first seen, so Lowell and others had to rely on drawings by astronomers of past centuries to compute the planets' orbits.

"Today most of us think that the old observations were not reliable," says Dr. Jane Luu. "The orbits of Uranus and Neptune don't seem to have the oddities they were once thought to have, which means that we have no reason to suspect the existence of a sizable tenth planet."

Clyde Tombaugh agreed with Dr. Luu, and he also added a personal reason for doubting the existence of a tenth planet. "I observed seventy percent of the entire sky and would have found it if it existed," he told me. "There is no such body as a tenth planet."

Nonetheless, just as Tombaugh continued his search after the elderly astronomer told him he was "wasting his time," so too a small number of scientists still believe in the residuals of Uranus and Neptune and continue to hunt for a large planet beyond Pluto. Among them is University of Maryland astronomer Dr. Tom Van Flandern, who worked with Robert Harrington in developing the idea of the tenth planet known as Humphrey. Van Flandern feels that the *Voyager 2* data did not settle the residuals issue, and he does not doubt the accuracy of the old-time astronomers.

"The old observations show systematic trends," Van Flandern says. "I still feel that there are residuals in the orbits of Uranus and Neptune, and to a lesser extent in those of Jupiter and Saturn." Van Flandern even thinks that "the orbit of Pluto may have residuals, too, but we can't tell yet." Pluto requires 248 Earth-years to orbit the Sun, meaning that since it was discovered in 1930, it has completed only about one-quarter of a single orbit. Incredible as it may seem, Pluto won't complete its first full orbit around the Sun since its discovery until the year 2178. "So we simply haven't observed Pluto long enough to determine if there are residuals in its orbit," explains Van Flandern.

The residuals Dr. Van Flandern finds in the orbits of Uranus, Neptune, Jupiter, and Saturn are just the beginning of his argument for the existence of a tenth planet. He believes more clues can be found by studying comets. Nicknamed "dirty snowballs" because their "heads" are balls of ice with gases, rock, dust, and metal frozen inside, comets generally lie beyond Neptune, but produce beautiful "tails"

The famous Halley's Comet.

when near the Sun. "I have studied the orbits of six comets, including Halley's Comet, that go out into the domain of where the tenth planet would be and that have returned to the inner Solar System," says Van Flandern. (Figures 19 and 20) "*All* of them show oddities as though some object we don't know about is slightly altering their orbits. My conclusion is that something not yet discovered is affecting the outer Solar System. I think it's a tenth planet."

Van Flandern points out several other oddities in the outer Solar

System—the objects beyond Mars that orbit the Sun. "Two of Neptune's moons are highly unusual. Triton, its largest moon, is the Solar System's only major moon that revolves backward [opposite to the direction of its planet's orbit]. Nereid revolves in a long elliptical orbit so far from Neptune [three and a half million miles] that it is about at the point of escaping from Neptune." Pluto's small size is another puzzle. Jupiter, Saturn, Uranus, and Neptune are all much larger than Earth. But Pluto has a mass (amount of matter) equal to only about one five-hundredth that of our planet. Another question is, what accounts for the Kuiper Belt, a band of billions of comets beyond Pluto that Jane Luu and her collaborator, David Jewitt, discovered in 1992?

Dr. Van Flandern thinks that the tenth planet accounts for *all* of these peculiarities. "I believe the planet has two to five times the mass of Earth and that its average distance from the Sun is several times the distance of Neptune. However, it has a highly elliptical orbit that causes it to periodically cross Neptune's orbit similarly to Pluto." By this, Van Flandern is referring to the little-known fact that for twenty years during each of Pluto's 248-year journeys around the Sun, the planet's orbit takes it closer to the Sun than Neptune. Between 1979 and 1999, for example, Neptune and not Pluto is actually the outermost known planet of the Solar System.

Long ago, Dr. Van Flandern believes, the tenth planet had a very close encounter with Neptune. "It disrupted Neptune's moons. One reversed its orbit and became Triton, and another was pulled out of its orbit and became Nereid. Two more moons that Neptune once possessed escaped completely and became Pluto and Charon. In other words, I think that Pluto and its moon were once satellites of Neptune. Perhaps after the encounter with Neptune, the tenth planet went out beyond Pluto and partially exploded, producing the Kuiper Belt objects."

Why hasn't Planet X (as the tenth planet is called, now that Pluto no longer warrants that title) been found? Like his late colleague, Robert Harrington, Van Flandern believes Planet X could be in the far southern sky, in a very starry part of the Milky Way. He thinks there are ways to locate it, however. Since William Herschel's discovery of infrared rays (also called heat rays), astronomers have developed infrared telescopes that detect and study objects by the heat they give off. Around the year 2001, the United States will launch the Space Infrared Telescope Facility (SIRTF). "The infrared observatory in space will have a good chance to find the planet because the object will stand out from the zillions of background stars more as a heat source than as a light source," explains Dr. Van Flandern. "If not found by the infrared telescope, there is an excellent chance that one day someone will look in the right place by accident and find it." In the meantime, Van Flandern is refining his calculations so that astronomers will have more of a clue about where to look for Planet X.

You need not be a rocket scientist to understand that old astronomical observations are vital to the Planet X debate, for if they are accurate, then it appears that a tenth planet really is pulling at Uranus and Neptune. Dr. Conley Powell *is* a rocket scientist—with Teledyne Brown Engineering in Huntsville, Alabama—and he is also a planet hunter who has studied the observations from past centuries. "The observers of old were more dependable than people realize," Dr. Powell insists. "I would not bet my life on it, but if you backed me into a corner and forced me to choose, I would say that the residuals are real and Planet X really exists."

Through a complex series of calculations, Powell has determined that the tenth planet equals two and a half Earths in size and is located five and a half billion miles from the Sun. Unlike Van Flandern, Powell thinks the planet is in the usual part of the Zodiac where the other nine planets are located. "Right now I think the planet is in the constellation Virgo. If we find it, I would like to name the planet Persephone, for Pluto's wife."

Dr. Powell says that taking new photographs to find Persephone may not be necessary. Instead, the planet may be waiting for someone to spot it on old photographs. "It could be on Clyde Tombaugh's old plates and should be bright enough to be visible. Tombaugh does not think he could have missed the tenth planet, and he clearly is a fine observer," admits Powell, "but anyone who examined ninety million star images could have missed one object." Dr. Powell did not want to spend years reblinking all of Tombaugh's plates, so he was currently doing further calculations to determine which particular plates should be scrutinized. He hopes that by the late 1990's he will have enough data to ask Lowell Observatory to blink the proper plates.

"If my calculations are correct, my Planet X has never affected Earth in any way and never will," Dr. Powell concludes. "The Planet X that some people think wiped out the dinosaurs would probably be a larger object and farther out. Both planets could exist."

The Planet X that may have caused the death of the dinosaurs involves some fascinating theories. If we view the Solar System as a family as Copernicus did, then the objects in its outer regions have long been considered distant cousins who have nothing to do with us Earthlings. What effect could comets, asteroids, or the outer planets have on us? What difference could it make to Earth if there is a tenth planet beyond Pluto? *Plenty* of difference, claim several scientists who believe that objects in the outer Solar System helped begin life on Earth—and could one day end it.

Every living thing on Earth needs water to survive. It has long been assumed that when the Earth was young, its oceans were formed by chemicals that rose to the planet's surface, and that organic molecules (the raw materials of life) were created in the oceans. "But it was probably too hot for water and organic molecules to have formed with the young Earth," says Dr. Daniel P. Whitmire, professor of physics at the University of Louisiana at Lafayette. So where did these substances come from?

From comets, Whitmire and others surmise. Today, nearly all comets remain in the outer Solar System. But when the Solar System was young, many more comets than there are now were flying about in all of its regions. Whitmire believes that billions of comets plunged into the inner Solar System, some of them striking Earth and providing it with water. Comets may contain organic molecules, adds Whitmire, which they deposited on Earth at the same time that they delivered the water. If this is true, we can thank comets for transporting the basic substances that began life on our planet.

Dr. Whitmire holds an even more startling idea: "Jupiter may be necessary for life's continued survival on Earth today by shielding us from comets. We could have thousands of times as many comet impacts on Earth if Jupiter's gravity weren't deflecting them away from the inner Solar System." Although water from comets may have been beneficial to the young Earth, we do not want these "dirty snowballs" slamming into our planet today, as two twentieth-century events demonstrate.

On the morning of June 30, 1908, a fireball fell toward Earth and exploded over the sparsely populated Tunguska region of Siberia, Russia. The fiery object was seen one thousand miles away and the blast was heard at a distance of six hundred miles. Fifty miles from the explosion, trees were ripped from the ground. Had the object struck a big city, the death toll would have been enormous. As it was, many reindeer and other animals were burned to ashes, but the loss of human life was small. One effect of the "Tunguska Event" was that it raised huge amounts of dust that circled the globe and caused unusual colors in the sky for weeks.

Scientists who visited the site concluded that an object from space weighing 220 million pounds exploded over Siberia with 2,000 times the force of an atomic bomb blast. Most scientists believe that the object was the head of a small comet, although some think it was a small asteroid.

The second event occurred far from Earth in 1994. (Figure 21) That July, Comet Shoemaker-Levy collided with Jupiter with such incredible force that the impact was visible even through small telescopes. Fragments of the comet that struck the planet raised giant billowing fireballs of superheated gas to heights of 2,000 miles. The impacts appeared on Jupiter's disk as dark spots that were actually the size of Earth. Anyone who witnessed the "Great Comet Crash" felt grateful that the collision occurred on Jupiter rather than on Earth, for the total energy unleashed was equal to *two million* atomic bombs. (Figure 22)

A comet like Shoemaker-Levy is believed to strike Jupiter about once every one hundred years. A comet or asteroid like the one that caused the Tunguska Event in Siberia collides with Earth about once every one thousand years. However, if giant Jupiter weren't there to gravitationally shield us, we would be struck far more often, perhaps threatening our very existence every few thousand years. One astronomer has nicknamed Jupiter "the Solar System's vacuum cleaner" because its gravity pulls in objects that could otherwise cause quite a mess on Earth.

Some scientists believe that much of the life on Earth *has* been wiped out repeatedly. Paleontologists (scientists who study fossils) have found numerous examples of animals and plants that seem to have suddenly disappeared. "It looks like mass extinctions occur on Earth roughly every twenty-six million years," says Whitmire. The most famous example took place sixty-five million years ago, when the dinosaurs died out rather quickly.

According to Whitmire and a number of other scientists, swarms of comets that strike Earth every 26 million years or so have caused the periodic extinctions. "The impacts raise up a lot of dust on our planet that blocks out sunlight," says Whitmire. "With less sunlight, vegetation dries up and lightning ignites fires. Large land animals die from the lack of food, the fires, and the acid rain that falls." This scenario is not just guesswork, insist Whitmire and Dr. Richard Muller, professor of physics at the University of California at Berkeley. A crater thought to have been created by one of the objects that wiped out the dinosaurs was discovered a few years ago in Mexico's Yucatán Peninsula. "Dinosaur Crater" was created, say Whitmire and others, by a comet's head with a diameter of about ten miles.

The next question is, what causes comets to smash into Earth every 26 million years? Professors Muller and Whitmire explain that there are two main possibilities: Planet X or a star or large planet known as Nemesis.

"I have long believed," says Dr. Richard Muller, "that an undiscovered star orbits the Sun at a distance of about three light-years." Muller admits that his theory shocks other astronomers, who have long asserted that Proxima Centauri, at 4.3 light-years, is the star nearest to the Sun. "The Sun's companion could be a red dwarf," continues Muller, referring to a small kind of star with a relatively low surface temperature. "These stars are very abundant and not very bright, but because of its relative nearness the Sun's companion would be visible in small telescopes and even binoculars." In recent years, Muller has become a star hunter as he has searched for the Sun's companion with a thirty-inch reflecting telescope. He has a name ready in case his star search pays off. "I call it Nemesis," he says, for the Greek goddess of vengeance, "because every twenty-six million years at a certain point in its orbit, the star causes catastrophes on Earth."

Nemesis doesn't harm our planet directly, claims Muller. Its highly elliptical orbit causes its distance to vary greatly during its

26-million-year trip around the Sun. At its closest approach to the Sun—hundreds of times Pluto's distance—Nemesis encounters the Oort Cloud, a swarm of billions of comets that is actually known to exist. "The gravitation of Nemesis disturbs the comets in the Oort Cloud and sends several of them on a collision course with Earth," says Muller. He believes that cometary collisions caused by Nemesis wiped out the dinosaurs and will continue to cause catastrophes on Earth at 26-million-year intervals.

Whitmire also thinks Nemesis is a possibility, but his version of the theory differs from Muller's. "I think Nemesis could be a dark star called a brown dwarf," he says. Nicknamed "star wanna-bees" because they never gathered quite enough size to set off the nuclear reaction that makes a star shine, brown dwarfs were first proved to exist in 1995 after astronomers spent more than twenty years looking for them. "Or I think Nemesis could be a large planet about the size of Jupiter," continues Whitmire. Currently he is studying fluctuations in the paths of comets to learn whether Nemesis is pulling at them. He hopes to determine the best parts of the sky in which to search for Nemesis, because he believes he may be able to locate the object with the infrared observatory that is scheduled for launch early in the next century. If Whitmire, Muller, or someone else finds Nemesis and it proves to be a large planet instead of a small star, it would be our Solar System's tenth planet.

Whitmire has a second theory about the 26-million-year cycle of mass destruction that specifically involves a tenth planet. The "Planet X" of Whitmire's theory would be much closer to us than Nemesis; and though it wouldn't be nearly as large as Nemesis, it would still be bigger than our Earth. "If it's there, I figure it is the size of from two to five Earths, and that it orbits the Sun at a distance of about ten billion miles [approximately three times Pluto's distance from the Sun] over a period of perhaps a thousand years."

Artist's conception of a tenth planet.

As is true of the known planets, Planet X wouldn't always follow the same path during its tour around the Sun. Whitmire figures the planet would require about 52 million years to undergo all its orbital variations. Twice during that time, or once every 26 million years, Planet X would pass through the Kuiper Belt of comets, which extends not far beyond Pluto and is therefore much closer to Earth than the Oort Cloud of comets. However, the mechanism by which Planet X would wreak havoc on Earth resembles the Nemesis theory.

"Planet X's gravitation deflects some of the Kuiper Belt comets toward the inner Solar System, bumping them toward Earth." In the end, several comets slam into Earth, kicking up the dust and starting the fires that cause the mass extinctions.

As Whitmire envisions it, Planet X would be much more difficult to locate than Nemesis. "I have no idea where to look, and I haven't found a method to search for Planet X yet," he admits. "It could easily be hiding against the background stars of the Milky Way, where it would be really hard to find. Yet it probably could be seen in regular optical telescopes—if you looked in just the right place." Whitmire thinks that astronomers searching for comets and asteroids may one day find Planet X by accident—or rather, to use William Herschel's words, by the "regular manner" in which they examine the sky.

It is possible to disagree with some of Whitmire's and Muller's ideas and still believe there might be a tenth planet, says astronomer and author Dr. Mark Littmann. "Most of us don't believe in the existence of a *large* tenth planet or in the twenty-six-million-year mass extinction cycle," says Littmann, former science communicator for the Hubble Space Telescope, which was placed in orbit above Earth in 1990. "Yes, perhaps sixty-five million years ago a comet or asteroid wiped out the dinosaurs, and perhaps there have been other mass extinctions from similar impacts. However, they didn't necessarily occur in cycles and weren't necessarily caused by Nemesis or Planet X." Yet, concludes Littmann, "although most of us do not think there is a large tenth planet, we see no reason why there couldn't be a small one."

Dr. Jane Luu of Harvard and Dr. Anita Cochran of the University of Texas are two astronomers who could discover the tenth planet—whether large or small—while looking for something else. Both study the Kuiper Belt comets that Luu helped discover in 1992. Like Dr. Littmann, neither Luu nor Cochran believes that a large tenth planet causes periodic mass extinctions by sending comets crashing to Earth, or that a massive planet beyond Pluto even exists. However, both agree with Littmann that there might be a small tenth planet beyond Pluto. "There could be another Pluto-sized planet out there that would have no effect on Earth whatsoever," says Dr. Anita Cochran. "Possibly there are a couple of Pluto-sized planets. Nobody is doing a widespread search specifically for a small tenth planet, but several of us who study the outer Solar System might stumble across another Pluto or two—if they exist and we happen to look in the right place."

But what if Professors Daniel Whitmire and Richard Muller are right, and every 26 million years Planet X or Nemesis bumps comets into the Earth, causing mass extinctions? "Then we are due for another catastrophe in thirteen million years," says Muller.

The blockage of sunlight, fires, food shortages, and acid rain caused by the cometary hits could condemn us to the same fate as the dinosaurs—if not for one thing. We can prevent the comets from striking our planet. (Figure 23)

"At eight thousand miles across, Earth is a relatively small target," explains Dr. Muller. "First we will need to figure which two or three comets out of the millions headed our way are on target to hit Earth, which would involve a great deal of astronomical work. Then we would go up to the comets when they are still fifty million miles from Earth and give them a tap to deflect them away from us.

"How do you take a comet the size of San Francisco and made of rock, ice, and frozen gases and give it a tap? When the comet is still fifty million miles from Earth, you explode nuclear weapons a mile above its surface, which will deflect it so that instead of hitting Earth it will only pass close." An interesting aspect of this plan is that most people are afraid nuclear weapons may one day be used to destroy the world. In this case, they would be employed to save it.

Muller's idea is not science fiction. We are already capable of sending up a space vehicle with nuclear weapons to change the path of a comet or asteroid. Even those who don't believe that Planet X or Nemesis causes mass extinctions can appreciate the value of this plan. Now and then random comets and asteroids strike planets, as shown by the object that exploded over Siberia in 1908 and the body that slammed into Jupiter in 1994. In the future, objects such as these could be deflected away from Earth by a "nuclear nudge."

TEN

THE SEARCH FOR OTHER SOLAR SYSTEMS

People who think Earth is the only inhabited planet have limited horizons. It's probably normal for stars to have planets. Some must be at the right distance and have the right conditions to support life. Even as we speak, there must be trillions of planets with alien civilizations on them.

Clyde Tombaugh

✸ At one time or another, nearly everyone asks the question: Are there other intelligent creatures in the Universe, or are we alone?

For centuries there was a popular belief that a variety of intelligent creatures inhabited the Solar System. Christiaan Huygens, a Dutch astronomer who discovered Saturn's rings in the 1650s, argued that all of the planets were home to intelligent life. Jupiterians were probably skillful sailors, Huygens claimed, because their planet had "so many moons to direct the course of seafarers." A century later, William Herschel reached an even more optimistic conclusion: Not just the planets, but even "the Sun is richly stored with inhabitants."

The existence of Sun creatures was disproved by 1881, the year our star's surface temperature was found to be 10,000 degrees Fahrenheit. Since the Sun is a rather typical star, it became apparent that no creatures, not even fire-breathing dragons, could survive on stars. At that point, people realized that there is something very special about planets, for they are the only places where life can exist.

Planets do not generate heat and light, but receive these forms of energy from the star they orbit. Mercury and Venus are hot because they are near the Sun, while Uranus, Neptune, and Pluto are cold and dark because they are far away from the Sun. All we need to do is look in the mirror to prove that a planet receiving neither too much nor too little heat and light can support life. Earth is home to about six billion people plus more than a million other kinds of animals and plants.

Until about thirty years ago, many people still believed that extraterrestrials might exist on one or more of the Solar System's eight other known planets. During the 1950s there was a popular saying that although they might not have "life as we know it," other planets might harbor "life as we don't know it." But starting in the 1960s, space probes (information-gathering devices) were launched to every planet except Pluto. (Figure 24) The probes taught us more about the planets in a few years than astronomers had learned in all of recorded time. For those eager to find extraterrestrials, however, the news was disappointing. Earth seems to be the Sun's only planet that has life today. The old idea that living things can arise on just about any kind of planet seems to be wrong. Most astronomers now believe that a planet must be somewhat similar to Earth to support life.

There is one glimmer of hope in the Solar System, though. Mars has no canals or cities, but it does have dry riverbeds. "This indicates that, long ago, the surface of Mars had liquid water, which every organism we know of needs to exist," says planetary scientist Dr. John Stansberry of Lowell Observatory. "Mars also seems to have lost a lot of its atmosphere over billions of years, so it may once have had more of the gases that life as we know it requires. Perhaps when Mars had more water and a richer atmosphere, it was home to life."

Recently scientists have discovered clues that Mars actually was once home to at least primitive life. In August of 1996 a team of sci-

Opposite top: This rock, found in Antarctica, is believed to have come from Mars, bearing evidence of primitive life on the red planet.

Opposite bottom: Tube-shaped structures found on the Mars rock may be fossil evidence that bacteria-like organisms once lived on the red planet.

ALH84001,0

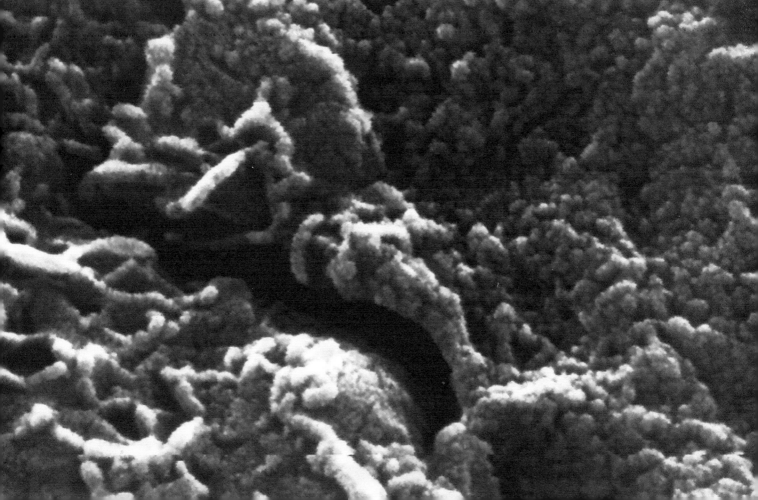

entists from NASA (the U.S. space agency) and several universities announced that an unusual rock found in Antarctica seems to contain microfossils—the preserved remains of microscopic organisms. Based on an analysis of the rock's chemical composition, scientists believe that it—and its microfossils—came from Mars. Fifteen million years ago, they say, a large comet or asteroid struck the red planet, sending the rock flying out into space. Eventually this piece of Mars hurtled to Earth, landing on the ice-covered continent of Antarctica, which surrounds the South Pole. The microscopic shapes in the four-and-a-half-pound rock resemble bacteria on Earth. If further studies prove that the rock does contain fossils of primitive organisms, it will be an "earthshaking breakthrough," explains Dr. Stansberry, for it will be the first evidence that life once existed on another planet.

Very few people think that the Martians Percival Lowell so fervently believed in ever existed. But if Mars was home to microscopic life-forms, perhaps animals and plants also lived there long ago. If that is true, says Dr. Stansberry, we could probably find their fossil remains, just as scientists on Earth have uncovered fossils of dinosaurs.

Scientists plan to investigate this possibility. Probably around the year 2005, the United States will launch a Mars Sample Return Mission to bring pieces of the red planet back to Earth. Around the year 2018, an event that human beings have long dreamed about should become a reality. The United States, perhaps in cooperation with other nations, will send astronauts to Mars. Among their activities, the explorers will dig for fossils. "What an exciting prospect!" says Dr. John Stansberry. "Imagine finding the first fossil fern on Mars, or the first fossil claw of an animal."

But the possibilities for extraterrestrial life do not begin and end within our own Solar System. As Giordano Bruno claimed four centuries ago, there could be "numberless Earths circling around their suns, no less inhabited than this globe of ours." Ever since the invention of the telescope, astronomers have tried to see planets orbiting other stars. Up until now (1997), they haven't succeeded, because planets thousands of times as far away as Pluto would be extremely dim and too near the bright light of their stars to be visible through today's telescopes.

Despite our inability to actually see planets around other stars, by the 1960s most astronomers felt that planets were common and that intelligent life was abundant. Their reasoning was simple: The Sun, a rather ordinary star in a rather ordinary galaxy, has at least nine planets, one of which has intelligent life. The average galaxy has many billions of stars, and there are many billions of galaxies, bringing the grand total of stars in the Universe to more than 50 sextillion (50,000,000,000,000,000,000,000). With all those stars, how likely is it that only the Sun has a planet with thinking creatures?

"Astronomers have figured that there are more stars than there are grains of sand on all of Earth's beaches," Clyde Tombaugh told me. "Even if just one star out of a million has a planet with life, there must be trillions of planets with extraterrestrials on them."

By the 1980s, calculating "Goldilocks Formulas" had become a popular astronomical pastime. These formulas estimate the number of planets in the Universe that might have intelligent life. A typical Goldilocks Formula begins with the assumption that a quarter of all stars have planets. It proceeds by figuring that one planet in ten is in the "habitable zone"—the area around a star that is neither too hot nor too cold but "just right" for life. The formula concludes by estimating that a tenth of all habitable zone planets actually have life, and that in a hundredth of those cases intelligent life develops. Without leaving our chairs, we have just figured that, as Clyde Tombaugh claims, there must be "trillions of planets" that are home to intelligent life.

There was a weak link in the Goldilocks Formulas, however. We needed to determine how common planets are. The conclusion that a

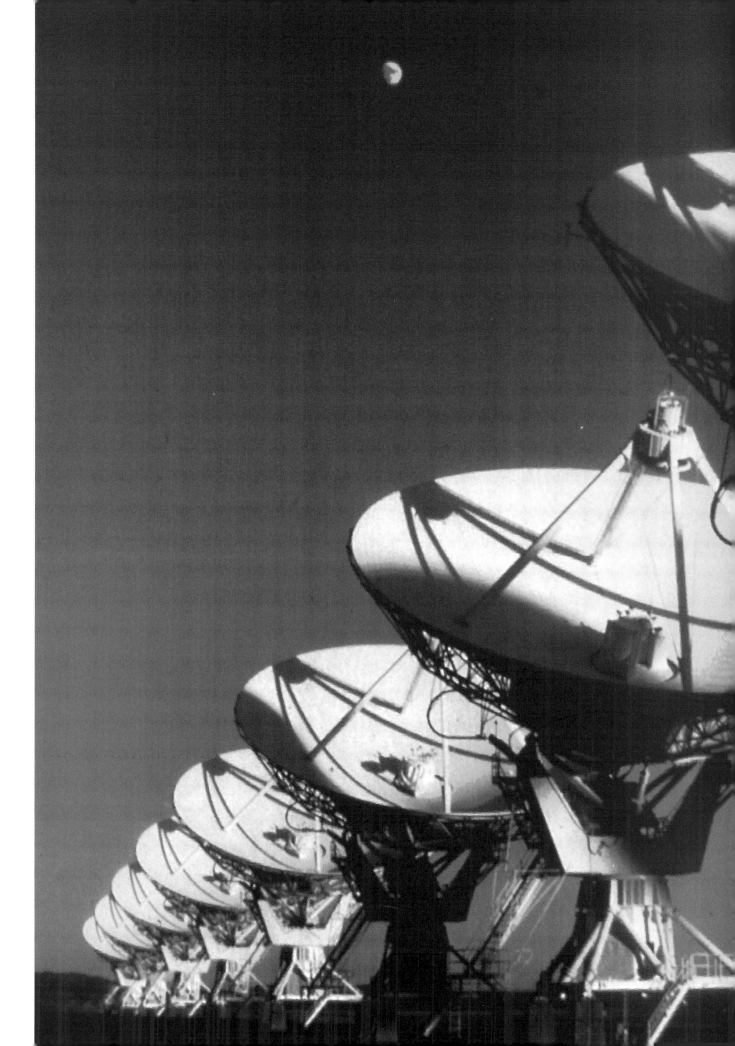

quarter of all stars have planets was little more than a guess. The true number could have been more or less—perhaps a *lot* less. It could have even been true that, unlikely as it seems, our Sun was the *only* star with planets. In that case, we would be alone in the Universe.

The question of how common planets are is related to another question: How are planets created? If they are a natural by-product of star formation, then planets are probably abundant. But if they are created by a very unusual set of circumstances, they could be incredibly rare.

For several centuries, there have been two main theories about the birth of the Solar System. According to the "passing star theory" (Figure 25), several billion years ago a star approached the Sun. So near did it come that its gravity pulled material out of the Sun that formed the planets and other members of the Sun's "family." If our Solar System began this way, there may be few planetary systems. Although they appear crowded together, the stars in the Milky Way are so far apart that astronomers think it would be rare for one star to approach another closely enough to create planets.

The other idea is known as the "single-gas-cloud theory." Billions of years ago, its advocates say, the Solar System began as an enormous cloud of gas, dust, and ice. (Figure 26) The gas and dust in the central portion shrank, generating so much energy that it became the Sun. Particles in the cloud's outer portions joined together to become the planets, their moons, and the other objects orbiting the Sun. Astronomers have long favored this theory, which has encouraged those who hope that planets are plentiful. We know that stars are born from clouds of gas and dust, so, since planets accompanied our Sun's creation, the same should be true of other stars.

The first evidence that planets really are plentiful came in 1983. That January the United States, Great Britain, and the Netherlands launched IRAS (Infrared Astronomical Satellite), which gathered

Opposite page: The Very Large Array radio telescope near Socorro, New Mexico, consists of twenty-seven dishes.

information on 200,000 celestial objects by analyzing their heat emissions. Among its discoveries, IRAS found that at least six of the fifty other stars within about fifteen light-years of the Sun, and several others at farther distances, are surrounded by disks of small particles. Due to the enormous distances involved, the precise nature of these particle disks could not be determined, but scientists posed three possibilities. In some cases, the particles may eventually join together and become planets. Although undetectable to us, planets may already orbit some of the stars, and the dust disks may be leftover debris from their formation. In still other cases, the dust disks may lack enough material to ever form planets. Because all three possibilities are consistent with the way we think our Solar System was created, the dust disks are clues that planets are probably common. Still, the 1980s ended and no object had been found that could definitely be identified as a planet orbiting another star.

This situation soon changed, thanks to some careful observers and a little bit of luck.

Objects in space don't only emit visible light. They also give off waves that the eye can't see, such as infrared rays and radio waves. In the 1930s, scientists began building radio telescopes to study the radio waves heavenly bodies produce. Since then, much more powerful radio telescopes have been built. These giant "dishes" have certain advantages over the largest reflecting or refracting telescopes, including the ability to penetrate farther into space and to study objects that optical instruments cannot detect.

Radio astronomers made an important discovery in the 1960s, when they located objects that emit periodic bursts of radio energy. Named *pulsars*, these incredibly fast-spinning stars send out radio pulses that can be detected each time they rotate. Typical pulsars spin about twice a second and send out radio waves so regularly that they have been nicknamed "cosmic clocks."

When he began studying pulsars, Dr. Alex Wolszczan (say it VOL-shtan) never dreamed that it would lead him into an exclusive club alongside William Herschel, John Couch Adams, Urbain Leverrier, and Clyde Tombaugh. Born in Poland on April 29, 1946, Wolszczan moved to the United States in 1983 and became a radio astronomer at Cornell University, which operates the world's largest radio-radar telescope, the 1,000-foot-diameter dish in Arecibo, Puerto Rico.

In early 1990 an unusual opportunity presented itself to Dr. Wolszczan. "The Arecibo Radio Telescope was broken," he recalls. Motors aim radio telescopes at the places astronomers want to study in the sky, but "the Arecibo dish could only be parked in certain positions because of necessary repairs," he explains. The malfunction proved to be a "lucky break" for Wolszczan. "The telescope was closed down for visiting astronomers, so [as a staff member] I had an excellent opportunity to use the instrument, even though I could only study parts of the sky not usually considered interesting. I decided to search for millisecond pulsars."

A millisecond is a thousandth of a second, and, as their name implies, millisecond pulsars rotate even faster than regular pulsars, completing one spin in several thousandths of a second. It is difficult to comprehend an entire star spinning hundreds of times per second, but Alex Wolszczan was about to discover something even more astonishing.

In February of 1990 Wolszczan found a new millisecond pulsar that was named PSR 1257+12 for its position in the sky. Wolszczan learned that this star was sending out a pulse once every 6.2 milliseconds, which meant that it was rotating 161 times per second. Millisecond pulsars emit radio pulses at such reliably regular intervals that, as Wolszczan explains, "they keep time comparably to the most accurate clocks people have ever built—atomic clocks." But there was something extremely odd about PSR 1257+12. At certain times its

pulses arrived a little early, while at other times they came a little late. When he discovered this peculiarity, Wolszczan thought to himself: "Millisecond pulsars don't behave this way!"

Wolszczan returned to Cornell University in Ithaca, New York, and went to work on the problem. Analysis of the pulses revealed that the variations were not random, but were repeated in regular cycles. Eventually Wolszczan determined that one cycle required 66.2 days, while another took 98.2 days, to complete. The question was: What caused this star about 1,500 light-years from Earth to change its pulse rate in regular patterns? "By the summer of 1991 I was getting excited because I was beginning to suspect what might be the cause," says Wolszczan.

Because the Sun is so huge and its gravitation prevents the planets from flying off into space, we tend to forget that the planets influence the Sun, too. But they do. The gravitational pull of the planets causes the Sun to wobble ever so slightly as it travels through the Milky Way. One day in the fall of 1991, Wolszczan had an exciting revelation. "I suddenly realized there was just one possible explanation for the figures I was seeing on my computer," he recalls. "I had no doubt that there were planets orbiting the pulsar." Wolszczan concluded that the gravitation of at least two planets was pulling PSR 1257+12 sometimes toward and sometimes away from us, causing certain of its pulses to reach us slightly ahead of schedule, and others to arrive a bit late.

Realizing that he had just discovered the first known planets beyond the Solar System, Wolszczan felt a little wobbly himself. "I had to get out of my office and calm down a little," he remembers. Wolszczan walked to the elevator, where he met a colleague. "I just found some new planets," Wolszczan told him.

"What?" said the scientist, certain that Alex was joking.

Wolszczan then explained further until the man realized that he was serious. "He was the first person to hear the news," Alex recalls.

Opposite page: Dr. Alex Wolszczan, discoverer of the first known extrasolar planets.

Each of the irregularly shaped objects in this photograph is a distant galaxy, composed of billions of stars.

Wolszczan and his collaborator, radio astronomer Dale Frail, computed the basic facts about the planets that were disturbing PSR 1257+12. In January of 1992 Wolszczan and Frail published their results in the journal *Nature*. They concluded that the 66.2-day pattern is caused by a planet about three and a half times the size of the Earth that takes 66.2 days to orbit PSR 1257+12. The 98.2-day pattern is caused by a planet equal in size to three Earths that takes 98.2 days to orbit the pulsar. Both planets are located at a distance from their star comparable to Mercury's distance from the Sun (36 million miles). Since the initial discovery, Wolszczan has determined that a third planet orbits PSR 1257+12 and that the pulsar may also have a fourth planet. Other astronomers agreed with the results and credited Alex Wolszczan with discovering the first known extrasolar planets (planets orbiting stars other than the Sun).

In late 1995 I visited Arecibo Observatory to learn more about this historic breakthrough. "The excitement here was absolutely incredible" after Wolszczan found the two planets, recalled Dr. Mike Davis, who was the observatory's director when the discovery was made. Standing in the warm Puerto Rican rain in sight of the 1,000-foot dish, Davis explained that life couldn't exist on the planets orbiting PSR 1257+12 because of the deadly X rays that pulsars emit. Nonetheless, the first discovery of extrasolar planets was one of the greatest scientific milestones in history.

"Not many of us doubted the existence of planets around other stars," says Davis, "yet there was still that small, nagging possibility that planets are rare. Pulsars are perhaps the last place you would expect to find planets, because they are the cores of stars that exploded long ago. The planets apparently formed from the debris left over after the explosion, which had been considered an unlikely way for planets to be created. So if there are planets around a pulsar, then certainly we can expect to find planets around many other stars."

Alex Wolszczan discovered a new planetary system because he was observant enough to investigate something out of the ordinary. His discovery has turned him into a planet hunter. "Now when I study pulsars and millisecond pulsars, I also look for evidence of planets," he says.

Wolszczan's discovery has inspired other astronomers to hunt for extrasolar planets, even though they can't actually see them. A few astronomers search with radio telescopes, like Wolszczan, and in at least two cases it appears that they have found planets around pulsars. But the main technique for searching for extrasolar planets involves attaching instruments called spectrographs to telescopes.

Made possible by Isaac Newton's discovery that ordinary white

RELATION BETWEEN RED-SHIFT AND DISTANCE
FOR EXTRAGALACTIC NEBULAE

CLUSTER NEBULA IN	DISTANCE IN LIGHT-YEARS	RED-SHIFTS

VIRGO

43,000,000

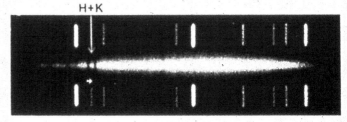

H+K

750 MI/SEC

URSA MAJOR

560,000,000

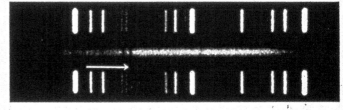

9,300 MI/SEC

CORONA BOREALIS

728,000,000

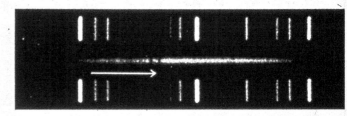

13,400 MI/SEC

BOOTES

1,290,000,000

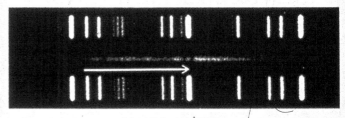

24,400 MI/SEC

HYDRA

1,960,000,000

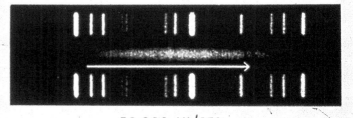

38,000 MI/SEC

light is actually a blend of various colors, a spectrograph makes a detailed record of the different colors in the light from a star, which is called its *spectrum*. (Figure 27) A spectrum of a star includes a number of bright lines that resemble bar-code stripes on store products. By analyzing star spectrums, astronomers can determine their temperature and chemical composition. Spectroscopy can also be used to determine if a star has a planet orbiting it.

The colors in a star's spectrum are the same as those in a rainbow, which is a spectrum of the Sun: red, orange, yellow, green, and shades of blue. The red waves are the longest light waves, and the blue are the shortest.

When the spectrum of a moving object is analyzed, the lines all shift to either the red or the blue side, depending on the direction of the motion. If the object is moving away from us, its light waves are stretched a little longer than usual before they reach the spectrograph, causing the lines to shift a little toward the long, or red, end of the spectrum (called the "red shift"). But if the object is approaching us, its light waves travel a little shorter distance than usual, squeezing the lines toward the short, or blue, end of the spectrum (called the "blue shift").

Astronomers hunting for extrasolar planets look for red shifts alternating with blue shifts in a star's spectrum, explains Lowell Observatory's Dr. John Stansberry. "This means that the star is wobbling, sometimes away from Earth, and sometimes toward Earth. This wobble in a star's motion is just what astronomers would expect if there were a planet orbiting the star, causing it to move a little bit."

Although searching for extrasolar planets with spectrographs is the best method we have, it has two limitations. For one thing, as with Alex Wolszczan's radio telescope studies, we cannot actually see the planet. Also, the method can only detect huge planets similar to Jupiter. "Using current instrumentation, we cannot locate an Earth-

Opposite page:

The spectrums of these galaxies display red shifts because they are moving away from us.

sized planet," explains Stansberry, because its gravitational pull would not be strong enough to cause a detectable wobble in its star.

In April of 1994, Michel Mayor and Didier Queloz of Switzerland's Geneva Observatory began a spectrographic study of 150 Sun-like stars in search of wobbles caused by planets. On October 6, 1995, Mayor announced that a star he and Queloz had monitored in the constellation Pegasus the Winged Horse showed strong indications of having a planet. Called 51 Pegasus, or 51 Peg for short, the star is fifty light-years from us but is similar to the Sun in age, size, and temperature. From the wobble they detected in 51 Peg, Mayor and Queloz calculated that a planet with about 60 percent the mass of Jupiter orbits the star at a distance of four and a half million miles.

Other astronomers investigated Mayor and Queloz's claim. They included Geoffrey Marcy and Paul Butler, who were running a spectrographic project to hunt for extrasolar planets at California's Lick Observatory. Using some of the world's best equipment for measuring star motions, Marcy and Butler confirmed the existence of 51 Peg's planet.

Like the planets orbiting PSR 1257+12, the planet of 51 Peg must be lifeless. It is so near its star that its temperature is estimated at 1,800 degrees F.—almost hot enough to melt gold on Earth. (Figure 28) Yet the discovery shook the astronomical world more than any event since Clyde Tombaugh found Pluto in 1930. Astronomers called it "one of the biggest discoveries of the century" and "one of those once-in-a-lifetime discoveries." The cover of the January 1996 *Sky & Telescope* magazine featured the headline NEW PLANET DISCOVERED! The magazine's article about 51 Peg's planet began: "A discovery that most astronomically minded people have awaited since childhood—one that many expected to go to their graves never seeing—has finally happened."

The PSR 1257+12 planets were discovered first. But what made 51

Opposite page:

The Keck telescopes

in Hawaii.

Peg's planet special was that it was the first one found around a star resembling the Sun—a type that we know can have a planet with intelligent life on it. If one Sun-like star has a planet, it seems likely that many others do, too, and that the conditions on some of those planets must be ideal for life.

Several more planetary discoveries soon followed, prompting jokes among astronomers of forming a "Planet of the Month Club." Like 51 Peg's planet, these planets were located when spectrographic studies revealed wobbles in Sun-like stars. In the first few months of 1996, Geoffrey Marcy and Paul Butler announced that they had discovered huge planets orbiting three different stars: 47 Ursa Major, 70 Virgo, and 55 Cancer. In October 1996 several astronomers, including William Cochran of the University of Texas, announced that they had discovered a planet larger than Jupiter orbiting the star 16 Cygnus.

By the spring of 1997, astronomers had detected at least ten planets around Sun-like stars. Detecting a few planets by indirect methods has convinced astronomers that the Goldilocks Formulas are right: about a fourth of all stars have planets. Astronomers hope that in a few years they will fulfill their old dream of actually *seeing* planets around other stars. One plan involves Earth-based telescopes. Keck I, the world's most powerful optical telescope, opened atop Hawaii's Mauna Kea volcano in 1993. A sister telescope, Keck II, opened next to this giant instrument in 1996. By about the year 2000, the two Kecks will be linked so that they will operate as one huge telescope system. Astronomers expect that, working together, the two Kecks may enable them to view Jupiter-sized planets in distant solar systems.

It would be a towering achievement to see giant planets around another star. But astronomers won't stop there, says planet discoverer Dr. William Cochran. "We are most interested in Earth-like planets, because we think they are the likeliest places to find intelligent life," explains Cochran, who makes a bold prediction: "In twenty years we may have the technology to not only discover Earth-like planets orbiting other stars, but to actually see continents and oceans on them."

We probably won't ever see planets resembling our own using a telescope on Earth. Our atmosphere distorts the view too much for us to spot such small worlds orbiting other stars. Nor are we likely to succeed with an observatory in orbit above the Earth, such as the Hubble Space Telescope, because dust in our part of the Solar System hampers our view. So how will we make Dr. Cochran's prediction come true? "By launching a telescope into orbit around the Sun in the outer Solar System," he says.

NASA is planning to build just such a telescope. Called the Planet Finder, it is expected to be launched into an orbit approximately 500 million miles from the Sun—roughly the distance of Jupiter. From that vantage point, beyond the atmosphere and dust that interfere with our view from on and near Earth, the telescope may be able to photograph Earth-sized planets in distant solar systems. Computers will relay the pictures to Earth, where we will be able to view them. The Planet Finder may be completed and launched sometime around the year 2015. "It should be able to tell us whether a planet has water and an atmosphere and whether the chemical composition of its atmosphere could support life," says NASA Public Affairs Officer Don Savage.

Astronomers who hunt for Jupiter-sized planets are laying the foundation for the Planet Finder mission, explains Dr. William Cochran. Currently in the midst of a twelve-year spectrographic study of twenty-six Sun-like stars in search of massive planets, Cochran reminds us that our Sun's planets range in size from gigantic Jupiter to tiny Pluto.

"So," says Cochran, "each time we find a giant planet, we identify a star that is a likely candidate for the Planet Finder to one day examine in search of smaller planets like Earth."

ELEVEN

IS ANYONE ELSE OUT THERE?

We are planet-based beings, and we believe that planets at just the right distance from stars with just the right conditions are the only places life can occur. So the whole story of searching for extraterrestrial life begins with finding planets around other stars beyond our Solar System.

Planet discoverer Dr. Alex Wolszczan

✳ What if in the twenty-first century the Planet Finder or another instrument spots a few blue-and-green worlds with oxygen atmospheres, oceans, and continents? Besides ranking as one of the most thrilling events ever, the discovery would mark the beginning of another scientific adventure, for people wouldn't be content to just *look* at Earth-like worlds. We would want to learn whether those remote planets were home to beings like ourselves.

There are three ways for us to communicate with extraterrestrials. One way would be for them to visit us. Tens of thousands of people have reported seeing alien spaceships or "flying saucers." Thousands of individuals claim to have been abducted or temporarily kidnapped by extraterrestrials. Although a few scientists believe these claims, most remain skeptical, for no one has produced a convincing photograph or other proof of visits to Earth by aliens or their spacecraft.

According to most scientists, the simplest and most sensible way to make contact with extraterrestrials (assuming they exist) is to exchange radio signals with them. For about sixty years, human beings have been broadcasting FM radio programs as well as television (which also uses FM radio waves in its operation). Some of the waves are received by our radios and TV sets, but others pass through Earth's atmosphere and travel endlessly through space at the speed of light—186,000 miles per second. A TV or FM radio program that is being broadcast at this very moment will travel a distance of ten light-years in ten years, twenty-five light-years in twenty-five years, and so on. If anybody on an extrasolar planet aims a radio telescope at Earth, they might detect our FM radio and TV broadcasts and distinguish them from the natural radio noise emitted by heavenly bodies. For one thing, signals beamed by intelligent beings are stronger than cosmic static. Also, our broadcasts are at specific frequencies, while radio noise from heavenly bodies covers many frequencies simultaneously.

With the proper equipment, the extraterrestrials could actually listen to our FM radio shows and watch our TV programs. If in our year 1999, extraterrestrials thirty light-years from Earth intercept our signals, they would receive our broadcasts from 1969. They might hear reports of the landing of the first people on the Moon on July 20, 1969, or watch that year's World Series between the New York Mets and the Baltimore Orioles. In other words, somewhere in space there could be intelligent creatures who listen to our rock-and-roll music and watch such shows as *Sesame Street, I Love Lucy,* and *The Three Stooges!*

Since we broadcast radio and TV signals, it seems likely that intelligent beings on distant planets do too. Several radio telescopes are currently being used to listen for signals from distant civilizations. These projects are known to radio astronomers as SETI, which stands for the *Se*arch for *Ex*tra*t*errestrial *I*ntelligence.

As of 1997, no alien signals had been detected. A difficulty with SETI searches is that there are millions of places in the sky to point our radio telescopes. It could take thousands of years to study each point in the sky long enough to detect an alien radio or TV signal. But if astronomers find a few Earth-like worlds, SETI researchers could target those locations where success seems most likely.

If we ever intercept broadcasts from another planet, we could set up a long-distance conversation with the extraterrestrials. We might teach them our language and relate basic facts about our planet. We could even beam them an encyclopedia of our knowledge, explains Dr. Mike Davis of Arecibo Observatory, the site of a SETI program called Project Serendip. The extraterrestrials might do the same for us.

Radio contact with extraterrestrials would satisfy our deep-seated yearning to prove that we have company in the Universe, claims astronomer Seth Shostak of the SETI Institute, an organization near San Francisco that is running a SETI search called Project Phoenix. "It would be scary to believe that in all of vast space, Earth is the only planet with living, thinking beings," says Shostak. "We humans need to know that we're not alone."

The possibilities of what we could learn from the extraterrestrials would be unlimited and "mind-blowing," says Dr. John Stansberry. For example, they might teach us how to end world hunger, cure cancer, and clean up our polluted planet. "Since the aliens are likely to be many thousands of years more advanced than we are, they might give us good advice on how to avoid war," says Seth Shostak. Planet hunter Dr. Daniel Whitmire adds: "We could learn information from them that would take us a million years to attain on our own. We might learn almost unimaginable science, such as the secret of immortality [living forever] for people, and how to travel to the stars."

The more difficult, yet more exciting, way to communicate with extraterrestrials is to visit them. Between 1969 and 1972 the United

States landed astronauts on the Moon six times. Around the year 2018, we will visit Mars. What will we do after we explore the Solar System?

"Ultimately our goal over the centuries is to visit planets around other stars," says Dr. William Cochran. "Today it is only in the realm of science fiction, but one day we may get serious about it."

The vastness of space is a major obstacle to interstellar travel (voyages to other stars). At the fastest speed achieved by people in space as of 1997—25,000 miles per hour—it would require more than 100,000 years to reach the Sun's nearest known stellar neighbor, Proxima Centauri, and far longer for more distant destinations. Obviously, if we expect to explore other solar systems, we must build much faster spaceships.

Rocket scientists have ideas for building spacecraft that can achieve speeds of millions of miles per hour, considerably reducing the travel time. They are known by such exotic names as the "fusion rocket," the "ion-propulsion spaceship," the "interstellar ramjet," the "antimatter starship," and the "laser-powered spaceship." Another idea is to launch an interstellar "space colony," a craft the size of a small town in which people would live generation after generation while journeying to another planetary system. Within the colony there would be houses, schools, parks, and farms. The travelers would live and die on the colony, until finally, after centuries, the descendants of the original space pioneers would reach their destination. (Figure 29)

Currently there are no plans to build an interstellar space colony or any other kind of starship. This is because of another obstacle to attempting interstellar travel. Few people want to spend a tremendous amount of time, effort, and money in building a starship as long as we know of no place to visit that might have intelligent life. But if we detect Earth-like planets, that will change everything, says Dr. William Cochran. "We would have a goal—to visit those planets—so it would spur our interest in building interstellar spacecraft."

Eventually, perhaps not many years from now, planet hunters will discover a few worlds that seem "just right" for life. Radio telescopes will listen for extraterrestrial broadcasts from those planets, and rocket scientists will start building spacecraft that can travel to the remote worlds. After studying several such planets, the day may come when we find one that is home to intelligent beings. (Figures 30–31) Then we will have solved one of the great mysteries in science and answered a question that has been asked since the first human beings gazed up at the five "wanderers":

Is anyone else out there?

THE NINE KNOWN PLANETS OF THE SOLAR SYSTEM					
PLANET	DIAMETER (IN MILES)	AVERAGE DISTANCE FROM THE SUN (IN MILLIONS OF MILES)	LENGTH OF YEAR (ORBITAL PERIOD) IN EARTH-TIME	LENGTH OF DAY (ROTATIONAL PERIOD) IN EARTH-TIME	MOONS
☾ Mercury	3,030	36	88 days	59 days	0
☾ Venus	7,520	67	225 days	243 days	0
☾ Earth	7,926	93	365¼ days	23 hours, 56 min.	1
☾ Mars	4,220	142	1.9 years	24 hours, 37 min.	2
☾ Jupiter	89,000	484	12 years	10 hours	at least 16
☾ Saturn	75,000	888	29 ½ years	10 ½ hours	more than 20
☾ Uranus	32,000	1,800	84 years	17 hours	at least 15
☾ Neptune	31,000	2,800	165 years	16 hours	at least 8
☾ Pluto	1,400	3,700	248 years	6 days	1

◐ BIBLIOGRAPHY ◑

Deem, James M. *How to Catch a Flying Saucer.* Boston: Houghton Mifflin, 1991.

Fradin, Dennis B. New True Books of the Planets Series (nine titles): *Mercury, Venus, Earth, Mars, Jupiter, Saturn, Uranus, Neptune,* and *Pluto.* Chicago: Childrens Press, 1989–1990.

Herbst, Judith. *Star Crossing: How to Get Around in the Universe.* New York: Atheneum, 1993.

Hoskin, Michael A. *William Herschel and the Construction of the Heavens.* New York: W. W. Norton, 1964.

Hoyt, William Graves. *Planets X and Pluto.* Tucson: The University of Arizona Press, 1980.

Levy, David H. *Clyde Tombaugh: Discoverer of Pluto.* Tucson: The University of Arizona Press, 1991.

Littmann, Mark. *Planets Beyond: Discovering the Outer Solar System.* New York: John Wiley, 1988.

Sheehan, William. *Worlds in the Sky: Planetary Discovery From Earliest Times Through* Voyager *and* Magellan. Tucson: The University of Arizona Press, 1992.

Tombaugh, Clyde W., and Patrick Moore. *Out of the Darkness: The Planet Pluto.* Harrisburg, Penn.: Stackpole Books, 1980.

White, Frank. *The SETI Factor.* New York: Walker and Company, 1990.

Articles on the Solar System and on the search for extrasolar planets appear regularly in *Astronomy* magazine (21027 Crossroads Circle, P.O. Box 1612, Waukesha, Wisconsin 53187) and in *Sky & Telescope* magazine (P.O. Box 9111, Belmont, Massachusetts 02178).

☀ CREDITS ☀

☽ INDEX ☾

Page numbers in italics refer to illustrations.

◗ L ◖

Dennis Brindell Fradin grew up in Chicago, Illinois, and earned a B. A. in creative writing from Northwestern University. He was an elementary school teacher for twelve years and is the author of over one hundred nonfiction books, ranging in subject from the fifty states to medicine to Native American history to astronomy. In 1989, Dennis Fradin was honored as an Oustanding Contributor to Education by the National College of Education in Evanston, Illinois. His special interests include astronomy and baseball.

Dennis Fradin is the author of *Hiawatha: Messenger of Peace*, which was named a Notable Children's Trade Book in the Field of Social Studies, and *"We Have Conquered Pain": The Discovery of Anesthesia*, which was a Junior Library Guild Selection, both for Margaret K. McElderry Books. Mr. Fradin is married to Judith Bloom Fradin, who helped him obtain the pictures for *The Planet Hunters: The Search for Other Worlds*. The Fradins have three children and live in Evanston, Illinois.